the
BOOKWORM
box

Helping the community, one book at a time

GOOD TIME

JANA ASTON

GOOD TIME

Jana Aston

New York Times Bestselling Author

DEDICATION

Kayti McGee,
thank you for being my emotional support kitten.

ONE

"MY COACH SAYS WE are the CEOs of our own lives."

Hmm. I like the sound of that so I keep listening. I've never been interested in CEO-ing anything, much less myself, but now that I hear it, it sounds right. Plus the advice is coming from a bona fide life coach, so it must have merit. I wonder if I should get a life coach? I bet successful people have life coaches. Happy people. People who have their shit together.

I don't have my shit together. If I had my shit together I wouldn't be stopping at a coffee shop to buy a muffin for dinner because I've run out of real groceries in the middle of the week.

To be fair, winging it has worked well for me thus far, but maybe I'm capable of more? Maybe I've got untapped potential I don't even know about yet? Maybe with the guidance of a life coach I could be that girl who has her shit together and wears four-inch heels on a Tuesday. With blown-dry hair and wearing a smart shirt dress with a slim belt, just like Meghan.

Fucking Meghan.

I usually braid my hair after my shower and let it air-dry until I get to work. Then I unbraid it before I get out of the car and tousle it with my fingers. I've got thick blonde hair and the braiding thing gives me a beachy look I get a lot of compliments on, but maybe people are simply being nice? I twist a lock of hair around my finger and hold it in my line of vision before dropping it. I eye Meghan's hair once again, wondering how it's still silky straight at seven pm.

I wonder if her life coach gave her a referral to a good hairdresser? I bet they did. I bet they give her all the best referrals.

The line moves and I shuffle forward, along with Meghan.

"My coach says I have internal resistance to living the life of my dreams."

Oh, my God. I have that too. I have that same thing. I've always been sure I'm on the cusp of living the life of my dreams, but then something gets in my way. Like reality. Well, that's settled then, isn't it? I definitely need a life coach. I wonder if Meghan will share who she's using? I can't imagine why she wouldn't, it's not like I know her, so we're not in a competition, but you never know. People can be so stingy with information. I stop twirling my phone in my hand and use it to look up 'Life Coaches Las Vegas' while I wait for Meghan to finish her call so I can ask her.

Oh, wow. There's like a million search results.

The Best 10 Life Coaches in Las Vegas, NV
Life Coaching Therapists in Las Vegas, NV
17 Best Las Vegas Life Coaches

That last one is weird, right? Seventeen? You don't stop a list at seventeen, it's just petty. I bet whoever made that list hated the life coach who ranked eighteenth so out of spite they ended the list at seventeen.

I feel you, number eighteen.

"Tonight we're going to work on shifting my internal blocks," Meghan continues, so I focus on listening to her while I click on the link to the article with the ten best life coaches, because I feel that too, about the internal blocks. I think. Except... except I usually do whatever the hell I feel like doing, so maybe I don't have internal blocks? Or maybe doing whatever the hell I feel like doing is blocking me from doing something better?

"We meet at that new Grind Me Café that opened in Henderson," Meghan tells whoever she's on the phone with, and my ears perk up, because that's where I'm at—standing in line behind her at the new Grind Me Café! When I saw the sign go up I thought it was a clever name for a sex toy store, but when I went in the first time I realized they meant grind like coffee beans, not like—well, never mind. It's a coffee shop—the very one Meghan is meeting her life coach at. And, not for nothing, they have excellent banana nut muffins, but the point is this must be kismet, which is a fancier word for fate but still means the same thing.

What are the chances that I'd be in the same coffee shop, in the same line, at the same time as a woman who probably maybe has some of the same issues I do?

The chances are low. Well, honestly I have no idea what the chances are but for the sake of argument, let's agree they're low.

Also.

The other thing is...

I bet life coaches are expensive. And we already know that Meghan and I have probably maybe some of the same issues. So. I should stick around and see if this life coach and I are compatible. Right? That makes perfect sense.

Meghan reaches the front of the line and moves the phone away from her lips long enough to order a medium black decaffeinated coffee, which is another thing we have in common, because I drink coffee too. With cream and sugar, but it's still coffee.

I place an order for the same thing and add a muffin because that was why I stopped here in the first place—to buy a muffin for dinner. Meghan probably had a grilled chicken breast for dinner with a side of kale because her life is coached. She's not flying by the seat of her pants and eating muffins for dinner because she ran out of Cheez-Its. Never ever. I take my time adding cream and a packet of sweetener to my coffee while Meghan finds a table and wouldn't you know it, there's an empty table next to hers. Luck or kismet? Hmm? Either way, this kind of opportunity cannot be ignored.

So I sit.

At the table next to hers, slipping a set of ear buds into my ears. I don't turn them on, obviously. They're just a diversion to make it less obvious that I'm eavesdropping.

That sounds so sordid—eavesdropping. It's more of a sampling situation, like when you go to the grocery store and they're offering samples. If Meghan didn't want me to sample her life coaching session she should have had it somewhere a bit more private, am I right? Besides, kismet has decided that

I'm meant to be here right now, sampling, and everyone knows you can't fight kismet.

I've no idea if I'm using the word 'kismet' correctly but I'm sure that's the spirit of it. Sure enough anyway.

I place the muffin on top of a napkin before I dig a pen out of my handbag and smooth a second napkin out for note-taking. I'm just a girl enjoying her own company with a cup of coffee and a muffin, incognito-ing like a baller. I stuff a bit of muffin into my mouth and resume the search for the best life coaches in Las Vegas while I wait for Meghan's to show up, because if tonight's appointment goes well I'm totally getting my own coach.

Except.

Oh, holy hot damn, life coaches are popular. Real popular. I sip my coffee and work my way through the top ten list. The website for number one claims they have a one-year waiting list.

One. Year.

I toss my pen onto the table and sigh. Like I'm supposed to wait an entire year to get my life together? I'm no expert in life-ing but that doesn't seem right. I move on to the website for number two, which claims they're not accepting any new clients at this time. I can't even get on the waiting list for number two.

Dumb.

Coach three is the same. I don't care for the vibe of coaches four and five so I don't bother checking their wait lists. Coach six is an attractive man who has no right coaching anything but my orgasms. So he's out because I'm not paying for that.

I like number seven but... wait. Wait one minute.

Is that price correct? I assumed they'd be expensive, but not *that* expensive. Who in the hell can afford that? Only a person with their life already together, that's who. Kismet is stupid. Why did it cause me to want a muffin for dinner, stop at this specific coffee shop and stand in line behind Meghan while she was blabbing loudly enough for the entire shop to hear her if I wasn't meant to get a life coach? Running out of Cheez-Its yesterday can't possibly have been a coincidence either—it was the catalyst for this entire sequence of events.

I stuff another bite of muffin in my mouth while I ponder what all of this means, but then Meghan's coach arrives so I decide to put my thinking aside while I focus on getting the most out of my sample appointment. That's the point of a sample, right? Maybe life coaching is the worst and kismet only wanted me to start blow-drying my hair. Might as well find out.

Fifteen minutes later I have my answer. I'm sold. Meghan's life coach is the best. She makes me want to be a better me. She makes me believe I can be a better me! I totally get why someone would want a life coach. I already feel calmer and more focused just from sampling Meghan's session! So... I know I should probably leave now. I should. But I still haven't solved the problem about how I'm going to pay for my own life coach, or even where to find one. It's not as if I can stand up now, stop at their table and ask for a business card, can I?

I cannot.

So.

I'll just stay a bit longer. A wee little bit. Or the entire hour.

It's the most practical thing to do. Normally practicality isn't my thing, so the fact that I'm willing to be practical feels like another sign, don't you think? I do. I think it means I was meant to be right here, right now. Besides, it seems like Meghan and I have a lot in common. If I was a few years older, had a better wardrobe, took the time to blow-dry my hair, and could afford a life coach we'd practically be the same person. Admittedly that might be an overstatement based on fifteen minutes of sampling her life, but we're similar enough. So it's kinda like she's helping her past self be her best self.

I pause and twist a lock of hair around my finger. Okay, yeah, that's a stretch.

I stay anyway.

The rest of the session is just as life-changing as the first fifteen minutes. We've worked on identifying our key strengths and identifying new skills we'd like to develop. And the thing is, it feels really good to identify my strengths. I've got a lot of great qualities. For example, I'm spontaneous. That's something Meghan is working on. I'm also really outgoing and great at going with the flow. Adaptable, is how Carol would classify it.

Next week we're working on decision-making skills. It seems that Meghan has made some bad decisions, but there's no judgment from me, because who hasn't? Besides, Carol said that oftentimes bad decisions lead to good decisions, because we learn from our mistakes. She also said that bad outcomes are not always the results of bad decisions. She said sometimes the right decision still has a bad outcome through no fault of your own and it shouldn't stop you from trying again.

7

I'm pretty sure they were talking about a condo she bought before moving to Las Vegas but the advice applies to all of the guys I dated in college as well. See how adaptable I am?

Carol is amazing.

Which makes me think, perhaps I should come back next week.

Because really, who's to say how long a sample should last? Not me. I'm not the sample police.

I'm just a girl, sitting in a coffee shop, capitalizing on my strengths. Unlocking my life's purpose. Expanding my comfort zones. Besides, this isn't even the worst idea I've ever had. It's not even the worst idea I've had this week, which is fine because bad ideas spark creativity. At least that's what Carol said, and I really like that outlook so I'm adopting it.

"Is this a good location for us to meet again next week?"

Yes. Yes, it is. Technically Carol was asking Meghan, but a coffee shop is really not the place for a life coaching session if you don't want strangers to benefit from the session too.

"I can't do Thursday next week," Meghan replies. "I'm out of town on a business trip. Let me check my schedule and send you an email."

Well, that's that then, isn't it? I'll never know when they're coming back and I can't very well hang out at this coffee shop on the daily like some sad novelist with an allergy to working at home. I eye a woman at a corner table mumbling to herself as she types. Definitely not.

"The only other opening I have is Sunday morning at eleven," Carol announces.

Problem solved.

TWO

"HOLY HELL, WHO is that?" I stop dead in my tracks, causing Mark to slam into me from behind.

That's not a dirty euphemism or anything, we're fully clothed. Mark bumped into me because he was too busy looking at his cell phone to watch where he was going. It might also be because I abruptly stopped walking, but the pedestrian always has the right of way, so whatever. Granted, the pedestrian rule is for vehicles and people crossing the street, not for co-workers in hotel corridors, but I've always been pretty good at adapting rules to suit my needs.

"Payton, Jesus. Watch where you're going."

"Me? You're the one who bumped into me!"

"Because you stopped walking in the middle of the hallway." He looks past me and waves at the empty hall to indicate how idiotic my dead stop mid-hall was.

"I stopped exactly because I was watching where I was going," I counter. "And I watched that guy"—I nod my head in the direction of the lobby visible from the second-floor balcony we're standing in front of—"and decided to stop."

"Watched that guy? Nice grammar."

"Mark." I pause, waiting until I have his full attention. "I need you to focus."

"Focused."

I really like Mark. I'm thinking about making him my work husband. It's early days because this is only my second week of work, but so far it's looking good. Sometimes when you meet the right co-worker you just know.

"Who is he?" I move closer to the balcony rail so I can better ogle my potential future husband. "The gorgeous one talking to Canon. Do you know? Does he work here?"

"No idea."

"We need to find out because I might marry him and have his babies."

"Really?" Mark questions, his voice filled with the undertone of not taking me seriously.

"Yes, really. It could happen. He looks like just my type. Tall, dark, handsome and hung."

"Hmm," There's that tone again.

"What? You don't think I'm his type?"

"I didn't think you were the type, period."

"What type is that?" I take my eyes off the gorgeous stranger to give Mark a glare. Just for a second though, because I can look at Mark anytime I want, and who knows if I'll ever see my maybe husband again.

"The serious type. The type who cared about getting married. Just yesterday you told me most couples would be better off setting a pile of cash on fire and using the flames to roast marshmallows instead of wasting it on a wedding."

"That's only because we were working on the Johnson-McNally wedding and that couple would be better off setting fire to a pile of cash than wasting it on a wedding to each other. They're both horrible.

Also, I was hungry and I wanted a s'more."

"Hmm."

"Besides, it's a well-documented fact that couples who spend less than one thousand dollars on their weddings are less likely to divorce."

"A well-documented fact, huh?"

"Your lack of faith in me is uncalled for, Mark. I know things."

"Sure, sure." Mark pauses for a moment before continuing. "Where is this information documented?"

"I saw it on a video in my Facebook feed."

"Your Facebook feed. That's real news, for sure."

"It looked pretty legit. It was a very professional video."

"Hmm." Again with the hmms.

"It could be true," I insist. "It sounds logical. Possibly."

"Based on that thousand-dollar rule every quickie marriage in Las Vegas should result in a long and happy union."

"Who says they don't?"

"Britney Spears, circa 2004."

"Wow. You're a real buzzkill, Mark."

"Thank you. That's how I introduce myself at parties. 'Hi, I'm Buzzkill Mark.'"

"I wouldn't lead with that. I'd save it for the end of the night when you're prying cups from people's hands because you want to rinse them out before recycling."

"Your imagination must be a very entertaining place to be." Beside me Mark props his forearms onto the balcony rail as he surveys the lobby with me.

"It really is, Mark. It really is."

"So how is it that you're in wedding planning if you don't care about weddings?"

"Stop saying that. We're in event planning. Event. Planning. Which sometimes includes weddings and sometimes includes better things that are not weddings." I've had enough of weddings to last me a lifetime. "I said I might marry that guy and have his babies. A wedding and a marriage are two very different things. I don't care about one day." I really don't. I care about forever and forever is unreliable, at best. Weddings are fun, sure. The fact that the majority of them crash and burn not withstanding.

"So one look and you're ready to spend the rest of your life with him?"

"Don't be ridiculous. I said I might, I never said it was a done deal. He might annoy the crap out of me if we spoke or, worse, be terrible in bed." Doubtful though. The man looks like he'd be a real good time in the bedroom. He's exuding sex and confidence and I'm not even in the same room with him. He'd be downright lethal if he was looking at me. "We might just have a torrid affair and then part ways amicably."

"Torrid affair? Who the hell talks like that?"

"I do," I say. "Just now. I just said it."

"Hmm."

"That's a nice suit, right? He probably has a real job, so when he divorces me he'll be able to pay child support. Do you think he looks like the type who would show up for their soccer games or would he just see them on holidays?"

"Your mind, Payton. Jesus."

"Statistically it's a fair question."

"Hmmm." Again.

"He's so pretty," I add wistfully. Like ridiculously good looking. Tall. Thick dark hair. Strong jaw. Olive complexion, I'm guessing Italian. That or he has a hell of a tan. He's in a suit that fits him like a glove. Broad shoulders, flat stomach. I know he must be packing some abs under that shirt. As I'm watching he raises a hand and flicks his wrist so he can look at the watch on his wrist. Call me crazy, but that wrist flick is my new thing.

"Tell him that when you meet. Men love to be described as pretty," Mark says drily.

"Gah, look at him though. I think he might be my kryptonite."

"You think direct exposure to him is going to weaken you to the point of death?"

"Hmm, no, that's not right. Am I not using that word correctly? Why are people always saying stuff like 'donuts are my kryptonite?' A donut isn't kryptonite, it's a gift to mankind."

"So you think that guy might be mankind's gift to you? Am I following correctly?"

"He might be. You never know."

"Well, he's leaving," Mark points out.

"They always do." I shrug, not bothered by this development. I keep watching though because damn, is he wearing that suit. I've got a bad case of the lust.

"Should we run downstairs and try to catch him? You can fake-trip into his arms or something equally stupid? I'd be happy to give you a shove."

"Nah." I step away from the balcony rail and start walking in the direction of the large ballroom. We were on our way to do a few measurements for the dreaded Johnson-McNally wedding when I got sidetracked. "You know what they say. If you love someone, set him free. If he comes back, marry him."

"That is not how the saying goes, nor is it relevant for a man you've never met."

"Says you."

"If I ever get called to testify against you for stalking I can't lie for you."

"You won't need to testify. Spousal privileges."

"We're not married."

"Not yet, but we'll be work-married by then."

"Work-married." Mark repeats the words slowly as if this is a foreign concept. "Will I know when that happens? Are these long walks down hotel corridors some kind of courting ritual I'm unaware of? Will there be a ceremony in the cafeteria when it's official so I know when our anniversary is?"

"Ohhh, a work spouse anniversary! I never even thought of that! See, Mark, that's why you're in the running. You're supportive and have great ideas."

"In the running?" Mark deadpans. "I've got competition for a workplace pseudo-marriage?"

"Not a lot, if it helps. And you're in the lead," I announce as I enter the ballroom, dodging a construction worker on the way. The hotel we work at has just barely opened. We're still in what we call a soft opening, meaning mostly travel journalists and industry executives checking into comped rooms. The casino floor is open for business, but the grand opening gala won't occur for another two weeks and most of the event spaces are still in the final punch list stage of construction. Paint touchups, chandeliers being hung, trim work installed. It's chaos and I'm loving every minute.

"Let's get these measurements done," I tell Mark. "I'm starving and it's meatloaf day in the cafeteria."

"Just go." Mark sighs as he waves me off. "I can do the measurements."

"Mark!" I beam. "You know what? Let's make it official. Today can be our work marriage anniversary. Congratulations. I hear that the traditional gift for a work marriage is a box of Cheez-Its. You can bring those in tomorrow."

"You did not hear that. You just made it up."

"I did, but to be fair, in order for anyone to hear anything someone has to start saying it to begin with."

"Right."

"I think it's got a fair shot at catching on," I add. "Far stupider things have caught on so it's possible."

"That's one way of looking at it."

"Trust me, I've got a lot of inventive ways of looking at things."

THREE

"DO YOU EVER THINK we should have been required to pass an adulting test before we were allowed to get our own apartment?" I pop a Cheez-It into my mouth while watching my roommate spread jelly on an English muffin.

"Um, no?" Lydia looks confused by my question as she wipes the knife clean before placing it into the dishwasher.

Okay, maybe it's just me. She is having an English muffin for breakfast while I'm having cheese-flavored crackers, so this might be a me issue versus a regular twenty-something issue. Still though.

"You don't find it the least bit concerning that we could eat chocolate Cheerios for breakfast every single day and no one is around to tell us not to?"

"Are chocolate Cheerios a real thing?" Her nose scrunches, her face lined with doubt.

"So real."

"Hmm." She takes a bite of her normal breakfast while I finish off the last of my Cheez-It breakfast—because the box is empty. I need to start buying the family-sized box or learn how to properly divvy up the amount of crackers I eat between trips to the grocery.

"Who would run the test?" she finally asks,

because she's a good friend and a good friend always considers your ideas before dismissing them.

"Mrs. Butterworth."

Lydia blinks several times while she stares at me. "A plastic bottle of maple syrup shaped like an elderly woman should be the judge of who is ready to adult?"

"Who else would do it? It's not like we could trust the government to make a fair assessment."

"That's probably valid."

We're both quiet then while Lydia thinks adult thoughts and I think about the questions I'd put on that test. Do I need rental insurance? How exact is an expiration date? Is it really that bad to eat cheese-flavored crackers as a meal?

"Are we carpooling today?" Lydia asks, sliding her handbag over her shoulder, keys dangling from her fingertips.

"Absolutely," I agree, grabbing my own bag and following her out the door. We work at the same place so sometimes we carpool. And today is Friday, so if we drive together Lydia won't be able to stop on the way home at a thrift shop, because that's how she'd spend her Friday evenings if I didn't intervene.

We were both hired at an on-campus job fair during our last year at LSU and it's sort of a big deal. Real jobs. Adult jobs with 401K plans and benefits at a brand-new resort on the Vegas Strip. My job is in event marketing so basically I get paid to help people plan events. Events that happen in Las Vegas at a fancy resort. How cool is that? I'm adulting like a baller, breakfast issues aside.

Lydia and I decided we'd share an apartment when we moved to Las Vegas, which is turning out to be a great decision because while we're the same age, we have very different skill sets. We're like two peas in a pod. If one pea was organic and one pea was fried and served with a side of delicious dipping sauce. Wait, no. I'm thinking about those crispy green beans at P.F. Chang's, so not a pea. Whatever, you get the point.

She's a brunette.

I'm a blonde.

She's a virgin.

I'm not.

She was a Girl Trooper through the twelfth grade and earned every life skill badge available.

I was kicked out of the Girl Troopers over a badge pyramid scheme.

It's fine. I didn't want to go anyway. Not really.

The point is, I'm helping her break out of her good-girl shell by encouraging her to live a little. Speak to the cute guys at the pool. Kiss the stranger at the bar. Earn all the fun badges, so to speak. It's a work in progress, but I think I'm making a real difference in her life.

We didn't meet until junior year in college and we never roomed together before moving to Vegas, or I'd have realized earlier that she needed my help. Event planning and helping people socialize is basically the same thing. At least it is when I do it. Or it will be. As someone fresh out of college I'm not working on the good events yet, but I'm having a great time on the projects I've been given thus far.

For example I'm currently organizing the rewards dinner for a chapter of the American Dermatology Association, who've booked a week-long conference next spring. I know, you think that sounds boring, but it's going to be real extra by the time I'm done with it. I'm working on a couple of weddings too, which are the worst, but I'm paying my dues. Eventually I'll work my way up to the really good stuff, like organizing launch parties for celebrity denim lines or a cosmetics conference. Events where I won't have to mediate between a bride and groom fighting over menu options and where to seat that uncle who won't shut up about politics while I bite my tongue about how stupid all of it is.

A wedding is just one day. One annoying day of trying too hard to have the best day of your life, which is impossible because the best days of your life are never planned. The best days always happen when you least expect them to.

"I'm worried about Rhys," Lydia says when we're about halfway to work.

"Why's that?" Rhys is her love interest. He's also her boss. And my boss. He's everyone's boss because he's the general manager at the Windsor, the hotel where we both work. They're not technically dating, but he's into her and he's fighting it, which is dumb because Lydia is amazing and they're going to end up together. Sometimes men just have to figure things out for themselves though.

"It's been two weeks since the, um, since the thing in the bar and I'm starting to feel like we're not going to happen."

The thing in the bar was an orgasm. In the back office, but still. I was super proud of her because that was way out of her comfort zone. When we got home that night I made her a bar badge, which is like a Girl Trooper badge for grownups. Dirty grownups.

"But also," she continues, "I feel like we're meant to happen. I cannot have all these feelings for no reason, can I?" She doesn't pause long enough for me to answer so I think the question is rhetorical. "I know he feels it too, I know he does. I just can't figure out why he won't act on it. He kisses me like he means it, Payton. No one has ever kissed me like that before, you know? It's different."

I don't know, because I haven't kissed Rhys. But I've seen the way he looks at her, so she's probably right.

"We'll figure it out," I promise her. "I'll ask around. I know people."

"You know people?" Lydia glances over at me while she's stopped at a red light. "We both started on the same day. Who do you know that I don't know?"

"Pfft." I wave off her doubt. "You're in human resources. I'm in event planning. Trust me, I get all the good gossip. No one is telling you anything."

"That's probably true."

"I'll have this figured out by lunch. It'll be fine."

"Do you really think so?"

"Probably. It'll probably be fine. I'll for sure have it figured out by noon, but Rhys might be into some weird shit for all I know. Like maybe he's into furry sex or something. Which is cool, no judgment, but I don't know if you're down for dressing up like a panda bear to get him off so it might not be fine for you."

"What?" Lydia shoots me another glance, her expression lined with confusion.

"Err, never mind." I don't think she's ready to know just how confusing dating can be.

FOUR

"ARE YOU SURE YOU want to do this, Lydia?" My superior socializing skills want her to say yes. Yes, because it'll be fun. Yes, because this is crazy. Yes, because we don't have anything better lined up for the weekend. But as her best friend, I want her to think this over. For those very same reasons.

It's Saturday morning and we're sitting in the parking lot outside of Double Diamonds. The strip club. Gentlemen's club. Whatever. The website didn't look nearly as seedy as I expected it to, but it's still a strip club. We're here because my best friend the virgin wants to go inside and ask the owner to help her auction her virginity. To Rhys, specifically.

I know.

It sounds too nuts to be true.

It's insanity.

But yet that's what's happening. I asked around yesterday and it seems that Rhys spends a lot of time at this gentlemen's club. And there were rumors of professionals. And by professionals I mean hookers. I relayed the information to Lydia at lunch and by last night she'd come up with a plan. The aforementioned plan of selling her virginity at some kind of auction, to Rhys. There is no way this plan is actually happening. Nada, zip, zilch. Lydia is the good girl. The good friend. The good daughter. The good everything. And this idea she has is nuts. It's not that I don't think Rhys will bite, he will. It's that I don't think we're about to encounter a strip club owner made of gold.

Anyway.

Into Double Diamonds we go.

I expect we'll be kicked out. Or arrested for solicitation. Or hogtied and tossed onto a plane bound for Mexico. What? I have a vivid imagination.

Instead we're asked if we'd like applications, which, I'm not gonna lie, is a little bit flattering. Sure, I already have a job, but you never know when you might need a back-up plan.

"I'd like to speak to the owner," Lydia replies, shoulders squared and head held high.

"Me too," I add, because I can't let her go back there alone, assuming the head honcho is here and we're allowed a meeting. Reason number one: I'm a good friend and a good friend would never send you into the back office at a strip club by yourself. Lydia is blinded by love and I can't let her make a decision she'll later regret. Reason number two: This has the potential to be real entertaining and there is no way I'm missing out. I stuff the application into my handbag as Lydia shoots me a look. I shrug—I kept the application because I'm curious, not because I'm actually going to apply. Probably.

We're escorted past a few elevated platforms with the requisite poles in the center, down a long dark hallway and through a door.

The door leads to... an office. It's a nice office. Really nice. It's quiet and a row of windows floods the space with natural light. There should be a view of the parking lot because we're a block off the Strip, surrounded by high-rise hotels and tourist traps. But instead there's a courtyard of sorts. It looks like a section of the parking lot was walled off and turned into an outdoor patio. The wall blocks out the view beyond from our vantage point just inside the office doors so all I can see is a flower garden and a fountain. A freaking fountain. This is super disappointing because I was envisioning a dark room with bad lighting and an overweight white man smoking a cigar behind a desk while a couple of goons stood at attention ready to protect him if the need arose.

Ahead of us there's a seating area with leather couches and a couple of armchairs. A coffee table sits in the middle, made of what looks like reclaimed wood set in a herringbone pattern, a slim metal frame supporting. There's a coffee bar built into the side wall—wooden cabinets topped with a slab of sleek marble, an industrial coffee maker and glass jars of sweeteners and granola bars lining the countertop.

And there's a desk.

Just one.

Where a curvy woman who must be in her fifties sits, beaming at our arrival, making me feel as though I've just stopped at a friend's house after school instead of into the back room at a strip club.

It's a bit of a letdown if I'm honest. I thought this meeting was going to be a bit more dramatic, but this woman looks like she runs a book club, not a strip club. The kind of book club that only discusses books with fade-to-black sex scenes or, worse, books with no romance at all. Ugh. Lydia doesn't need me here for this. These two will be exchanging crockpot recipes while they sort out Rhys' life for him with this pseudo-auction.

I hate not being needed.

"I'm Sally," the woman says, rising from her desk with another smile. "You ladies wanted to see Vince? Can I offer you a coffee or water before you go in?"

Vince. Okay, now we're talking. Vince sounds like he could be a goon smoking a cigar. Vince could be sitting in a dimly lit office that smells like desperation and looks like the set of a mafia drama on HBO.

"No, I'm fine, thank you," Lydia says, politely declining the beverage offer.

"I'm good too," I add, holding up my half-empty iced coffee cup, rattling the ice with a shake of my wrist. "Still working on this, thank you."

The woman nods and moves around her desk, gesturing towards a closed door as she walks. Reaching it, she opens it and waves us through, telling Vince we're the young ladies who requested to see him. The door shuts softly behind us.

This is it. The office. The head honcho.

There's no smoke.

No goons.

And Vince? Vince is not who I was expecting. Not even close.

FIVE

HOLY MOTHER OF shit. Vince is hot. Young and hot. Well, not that young—I'd guess he's in his thirties, but I was expecting a fat man in his seventies, so he's young comparatively. He's also the same man I saw in the lobby of the Windsor a few days ago, talking to Canon.

Which means he's come back to me, doesn't it? I think it does. Sure, it could be a coincidence. It could. Canon is friends with Vince, so he stopped by the hotel. Lydia likes Rhys, so we stopped by the strip club. Blah, blah, blah. Coincidence? Nope. Because coincidence is really just another word for fate. It's true, look it up.

I grin. Big, big, big.

I've never had a thing for older guys. I've never been that girl who fantasized about seducing her teacher or her coach or her older brother's best friend. I've never fantasized about seducing anyone really, mainly because in my experience boys haven't been that hard to get. I've always dated guys from school and it was always easy enough to determine if there was a mutual attraction before I got too invested in crushing on someone.

Vince is delicious. Vince is every inappropriate fantasy I've never had wrapped up into one package.

This day is already going so much better than I could ever had anticipated. Maybe Lydia's plan isn't so nuts after all. See! Another coincidence! Who sells their virginity? No one, that's who. Especially not twenty-two-year-old women with jobs and a history of being good girls.

Yet here we are.

Vince glances up from his desk as Sally announces our arrival and when his eyes land on mine they're just as devastating as I knew they would be, except I don't think devastating is the right word. I need to thesaurus myself another word for his eyes later. A word that means I want to have his babies immediately.

Maybe. It's still possible he'll annoy me when he speaks, so there's no need to get ahead of myself. No worries though, if we don't click, we can still have sex. As long as he's willing to shut the fuck up.

I wonder what he's into? He runs a gentlemen's club so I might need to be open to new things, but I've always prided myself on my adaptability so I feel good about this.

Lydia strides forward and sticks her hand out in introduction. Bless her heart. If she prepared a presentation for this meeting I will die. I stroll up beside her as Vince rises and shakes her hand, a look of polite indifference on his face. He doesn't even check out her tits.

This is nothing like the meeting I was expecting.

"Payton," I tell him, holding out my hand when Lydia is done. His gaze flickers from her to me as he shakes my hand. He doesn't check out my tits either, which is disappointing. Gentlemanly but disappointing nonetheless. They're really nice, my tits. To be fair though, I did dress for a meeting with

28

an old pervert, not one with my maybe future husband.

This office looks much the same as the reception area we were just in. Expensive neutrals. A wood desk that looks like it would be comfortable on the pages of a high-end furniture catalog. Two sleek chairs placed before it for visitors and a credenza behind with a single potted plant on the surface. I'm guessing that touch is Sally's.

It's a nice office. Polished, much like Vince himself.

There's not even a casting couch.

We sit, Vince flicking his wrist to check the time on his watch and announcing that we have fifteen minutes.

I glance at Lydia, waiting for her to start but she looks like she wants to throw up. No worries, that's why I'm here. I'll distract Vince until Lydia pulls herself together. By distract I mean I'll get to know him better.

"Do you have multiple girlfriends?" I ask.

"Excuse me?" Vince's expression barely changes, like at all. He focuses on me, head tilted a fraction in my direction, but I know he heard me. It's not even that weird of a question considering where we are.

"You know, like Hugh Hefner did?"

His eyes narrow now, just a bit, as he sizes me up. I try not to smile.

"I run a gentlemen's club in Vegas, not a lifestyle magazine," he replies after a moment, refuting my question without really answering it.

"Same thing." I shrug and shake my head. The movement causes a lock of hair to tumble into my face so I twist my lips and blow it away with a huff as I bring the cup of iced coffee to my lips, pausing before I take a sip. "Anyway, do you?" I shake the cup to stir what's left of my drink, an unnecessary habit causing the ice to rattle against the sides.

Vince's gaze flicks from the cup to my lips as I take a sip. I suspect the ice-rattling will drive him nuts before we've reached our first anniversary.

I rest my forearm over the arm of the chair, the cup dangling from my fingertips as I settle back into the chair. It's a very comfortable chair. I wonder if the girls sit here to negotiate raises. Then I wonder if strippers get raises. They should, but I'll ask later because I don't want him to think I'm going to tell him how to run his business on our first date. I probably will tell him how to run his business, but that's besides the point.

Vince is silent and Lydia is still fidgeting in the chair beside mine so I fill the void by explaining why we're here. I tell him that Lydia is in love with Rhys and that Rhys is going to fall in love with Lydia if he's not already and then she'll move in with him and I'll have to get a new roommate.

I know the roommate concern is selfish but it is a worrisome thought. Living with Lydia is like having Mary Poppins for a roommate, she's practically perfect in every way. I'll never be able to find another roommate to fill her shoes, so to speak, so it's going to suck when she moves out. And she will, I know she will. Rhys is going to fall for her and whisk her off and then I'll be alone.

Unless I replace her with Vince.

I realize this is a leap, but fate is a capricious bitch and who am I to doubt her?

Plus I'd like to have sex with Vince so there's that.

I can't imagine he'd want to move into my apartment in Henderson, but that's okay because I'm sure he has a nicer place than I do and sometimes you have to make compromises. People often use the word 'compromise' when they're actually getting everything they want. Like me, right now.

"I could be your third girlfriend," I offer. Hef had three girlfriends, maybe Vince has a mansion filled with girlfriends too? I might be okay with that. I mean, I can't know for sure unless I try it, right? I'm a pretty independent woman so I think I could be cool with a timeshare boyfriend. If there were three of us I'd still get him two point three nights a week. I'd use the remaining nights to have dinners with my friends or wax my legs or catch up on episodes of *Love Island*.

Unless he has seven girlfriends. I need more than one night of attention per week.

"I'd be open to being girlfriend number three," I clarify, just in case he's got seven. "I don't want to be girlfriend one or two, it sounds like too much responsibility, you know? Also I'd like my own room. Is that how you do it? Do the girlfriends all get their own rooms? That's how Hef did it. Do you have a nice place? Because I'm not sharing you if you live in a shitty condo with coin-operated laundry."

That's the thing, isn't it? Hugh Hefner without the mansion would have been weird. Exceptions were made for Hef because of the mansion and the parties and the room service. Can you imagine living in a house where you could call the kitchen and order food delivered to your room? I can. I can imagine it. Because I saw it on an episode of that show Hef did with his girlfriends.

Or what about that show where a bunch of women compete for the same guy at the same time? In what world does that happen? One guy dating twenty-eight women at the same time? While they all live in the same house? That shit would not fly on a college campus, I can assure you. Not even if each girl had her own room and the guy was the star of the football team. Nope. But stick everyone inside of a beachfront estate in Malibu and suddenly it's normal.

I should probably watch less reality television.

"Are you serious?" Vince blinks twice and his expression isn't exactly neutral anymore. I'm not sure what he's feeling but it's okay, because he's definitely feeling something and that's really all that matters. I've stirred feelings in him. It may be agitation versus arousal but it's a start. Besides, I bet he'd be great at the hatefuck. God help me, why is he so attractive?

"Serious as a shark," I tell him while I try to block out the image I've just created in my head of him tying my hands together with a tie and bending me over that desk.

I know, I know. He's not even wearing a tie. Damn my overactive imagination.

"That's not even a thing," he responds, picking up a mug from his desk and leaning back in his chair as he takes a sip, eyeing me over the rim. "The saying is serious as a heart attack."

"Like sharks aren't serious? You try swimming with a shark and then tell me how not-serious they are." I rattle my ice and take another sip, confident I've made my point.

"You know he slept with all of them, right?"

"Duh," I reply. I'm not an idiot.

"You're really something, aren't you?" Vince asks, setting the mug down on his desk and leaning forward, arms braced on the desk. He's wearing a white oxford shirt, no tie. I find the choice very compelling for a Saturday morning. Most men would be in a t-shirt. The sleeves are rolled back to his elbows and I find this sexy as all hell. The top couple of buttons are undone and I can see a hint of his chest and if I thought he'd allow it, I'd crawl into his lap right now and work my way through the rest of those buttons. I know this isn't the time or place and that my insta-lust defies reasonableness but he just does something for me. Something primal. Something wanton. He's even better-looking up close than he was from my vantage point on the balcony a few days ago.

"I'm a lot of things. It's true," I agree. I bet this is exactly what my life coach meant about capitalizing on my strengths. I feel good about all of this.

"Payton, was it?" he questions and I beam. He remembers my name. Granted, I only gave it to him three minutes ago, but I like a man who pays attention. It bodes well for his skills in bed.

"Yeah?" Big smile. I know I've done most of the talking thus far but I'd say it's going well and my lust crush is still a hundred percent on. Vince looks like a real good time and that's what I'm after. A good time is a great place to start and maybe it'll lead to something more, maybe it won't. Likely it won't because he owns a strip club and I've got issues.

"Why are you here?"

Ugh, Vince. That was rude. I literally just explained why I'm here. Of course, I suppose that was an explanation of why Lydia is here, wasn't it? I didn't explain what I'm doing here, did I? It's not as if I planned to come here with an offer to be his girlfriend, because I didn't even know he was going to be here. That was all fate.

"I'm earning my best friend badge," I offer with a small shrug. I wouldn't mind a best friend badge, actually. I lost the few badges I had during the badge pyramid débacle.

"Vince," Lydia interrupts, finally gathering the courage to take charge of this meeting, which is a good thing because I'm pretty sure Vince is contemplating booting us out of his office. "I have a proposition for you."

"I'm listening, Miss Clark," Vince replies, his gaze sliding away from mine as he focuses on Lydia. "You've got nine minutes left. If you want something you'd better get to it. Quickly."

This is the part where Lydia blurts out her plan. The part where she asks the owner of a strip club—a man she's never met before—to auction off her virginity. But only if Rhys is the winning bidder.

Good Lord, how did I allow her to leave the apartment with this idea? I do not deserve a best friend badge.

When she finishes Vince stares at her in complete silence, his fingers drumming on the desktop. Crap, this is kinda tense. I hate tension. I take a nervous drag from my iced coffee but it's empty so the room fills with that annoying hollow rattling noise that occurs from creating a wind tunnel in an empty cup. That and the sound of me shaking the ice against the side. Vince glares at me, but I attempt another sip in case the ice-shaking freed a few drops. It didn't.

"Are you for real?" Vince asks, eyes firmly on mine.

"So real. And so are my boobs." Which he has yet to look at. I'm never wearing this top again. The man makes his living running an establishment with topless women and he can't even be bothered to check out my rack? It's insulting. And bad business. My tits are phenomenal. He should make a note of that in case I ever do submit an application. Jerk.

He stares at me another moment before shaking his head with a single nod as he turns his attention back to Lydia. "This isn't a brothel," he tells her. "Prostitution isn't legal in Clark County."

"Of course not," she agrees hurriedly. "Double Diamonds is a business though, isn't it, Mr...?"

"Vince," he replies, deadpan.

"Right. Mr. Vince, you're a businessman at heart, aren't you? So let's make a deal. I'll make it worth your while," Lydia promises.

God, this girl. A basket of fresh-baked cookies is not going to make this worth his while. She is so out of her league.

"Scout's honor," I volunteer as I give Vince a wink, a big dramatic wink complete with a head tilt and a click of my tongue. "The Urban Dictionary kind, big guy."

Lydia's head turns towards me and now she's glaring at me too. Sheesh, you try and help a friend out! It's not as though I was volunteering her for sexual favors. No way I'd volunteer her, Vince is mine and I'm already sharing him with those two other girlfriends. Wait, he never confirmed that, did he? Huh, he's really not very forthcoming with the personal information. He's not wearing a ring, but maybe he's already got a girlfriend. A real one whom he loves and doesn't fuck around on.

Lucky girl.

Vince leans back in his chair, running two fingers across his lips while he watches us with newfound interest. "So you work at the Windsor. Both of you?"

We nod.

"Let's talk terms."

And that is the story of how a virgin convinced the owner of a gentlemen's club to help her, and she lived happily ever after.

But it's not my story.

SIX

I LEAVE LYDIA AT Double Diamonds and drive back to our apartment alone. One of the strippers from the club is giving her a tour, then they're going shopping to find Lydia something to wear tonight before she has her hair and makeup done.

My little girl is all grown up.

I'll go back tonight before the auction to support her. Double-check that she really wants to do this. Triple-check that she understands there's no blowing in blow jobs. All the regular best friend duties.

I flip the visor down to block out the sun as I turn into our apartment complex and the invitation I tucked up there a few days ago falls out and hits me in the face.

A wedding invitation. For less than a month from now. I'm no etiquette expert but I don't think that's right. Especially when it's your mother's wedding. It is her third though, so maybe the social parameters of wedding invitations get more lax with each progressive union? I believe this is her fiancé's third wedding as well. They have so much in common, after all.

Spotting an open parking spot in front of our building, I pull in but don't turn off the engine. I have nothing to do today and I don't feel like going inside alone, which is stupid. I'm perfectly capable of entertaining myself, always have been, so I don't know why I'm so unsettled today.

Vince.

Vince is why.

Vince has me all kinds of worked up and I'm really looking forward to seeing him again later.

I will see him tonight, won't I?

God, what if he doesn't even work on Saturday nights? Wait, that's stupid, he owns a strip club, surely he works on Saturday nights. Except he was there this morning, too. I bet he's a hard worker. Fuck, that's hot. Even if he's working hard peddling tits and ass, it's important to take pride in what you do.

I find the idea of him very exciting. He's the ultimate bad boy and that turns me all kinds of on. I know I should be focusing on finding a good guy, but the bad ones are just so delicious.

I think we're meant to be.

By meant to be, I mean in bed. Meant to be in bed.

Having sex.

Or on the couch. His desk. I don't really care where as long as that beautiful man's lips are pressed somewhere against my body.

And then maybe we'll date and I'll live out my bad boy fantasies. I'll take pole-dancing lessons and give him a private show. We'll have sex at the club in his office. He'll take me for a ride on his motorcycle. Or maybe I'll never see him again, who knows. I can't even picture him on a motorcycle so it's a bit of a rough draft fantasy.

Good thing I'm flexible. I should remember to mention that.

I tap my fingertips against the steering wheel while I think. I hope he's agreeable to my sex plan, by which I mean my plan to have crazy hot, no-strings-attached sex with him this weekend. I can't imagine why he wouldn't be agreeable because it's a good offer, but I don't know him well enough to know, do I? I know almost nothing about him, other than he was much nicer than he had to be today, to both Lydia and myself. And that he's attractive. Really, really attractive. Also, I'm fairly certain I caught his eyes on my ass when I glanced back to get one last look at him on the way out of his office earlier, so that's something. Clearly he's an ass man as it's the only logical explanation for his lack of interest in my tits.

But he is interested.

Maybe.

I turn off the car and head inside because I'm not going to resolve anything sitting in the parking lot. Besides, my options for the day are clear. I can go shopping, find a gift for my mother's upcoming wedding and knock that off my to-do list. Or I can focus on Vince.

The choice is pretty clear.

SEVEN

THE LOCKER ROOM at Double Diamonds reminds me of a spa. Changing rooms, showers and a long vanity for applying makeup. There are a few rows of lockers tucked around a corner, but no jarring slap of metal when they open and close because they're made of wood and must have soft-close hinges because I've yet to hear one of them snap shut.

Just inside the door is a seating area. Club chairs surround a round coffee table. A couple of high-backed wing chairs sit against the far wall with a shared ottoman between them. There's a coffee station in here too, one similar to the setup in Vince's office. Mini glass-fronted refrigerators line the countertop beneath, filled with an array of bottled water, energy drinks and soda. There's even a fruit basket on the coffee table. The only things missing are fluffy white robes with an embroidered Double Diamonds patch.

I've never been in a strip club before, but this cannot be normal. The front looked and felt exactly like anyone would expect a strip club to look and feel. Loud and dark. Strobe lights flashing and beautiful women dancing. Glasses clinking and music thumping. The back room doesn't match my expectations at all. It's serene, peaceful. Quiet. There was some money put into soundproofing between the front-of-house and back-of-house areas here, that's for sure.

Nothing behind the scenes at Double Diamonds has been what I expected.

I drop my handbag onto one of the chairs and walk over to where Lydia is sitting in front of a makeup mirror at the vanity. The locker room is surprisingly empty too. Or maybe it's not surprising, it just wasn't what I was picturing. I can hear a shower running and I passed a girl exiting the locker room as I entered, but I'd imagined a room filled with half-naked girls rushing around and maybe some bickering about who got the good pole tonight.

I really need to get my imagination in check.

"You look gorgeous, babe," I tell Lydia as I approach. She does too. Rhys is done for.

"You look nice too," Lydia comments, eyeing me in the mirror.

"Do I?" I glance down at myself in fake surprise, as if it's some kind of fluke that I look good tonight. It's not. I took a shower and washed my hair for the second time today just so I could properly blow it out until it was silky straight. I've got really thick blonde hair, so the whole blow-dry-to-perfection thing doesn't happen every day. Nor does moisturizing from head to toe and painting my lips the perfect shade of fuck-me pink. Or pairing a body-hugging low-cut top with low-rise jeans that fit my ass perfectly. And fine. Fine. I might have added a a bit of body shimmer to highlight my cleavage.

"Are you going to Hennigan's later?" Lydia questions, referring to a bar near our apartment, clearly still trying to figure out why I've taken so much effort to get ready tonight when she's the one going up for auction.

"Um, I don't know, maybe?" I hope not. "So, what's the plan? Is Rhys here yet? Are you positive you want to do this, Lydia?"

"Yeah, I'm doing this. Assuming Rhys shows up, I'm doing this. He just does it for me, Payton. I think he might be my swan." I swear to God little hearts float over her head as she tells me about how swans mate for life because they choose carefully.

I think I might be a porcupine. I read something once about how the female porcupine lures the male porcupines to her, selects one but then makes him wait until she's good and ready before presenting herself for sex. Once she's had enough she tells the male porcupine to fuck off because she'd rather be alone. I'm paraphrasing obviously, but you get the gist.

Lydia's a monogamous swan.

I'm a persnickety porcupine.

"In case we don't get to talk later, I'm really proud of you, Lydia." I pull her to me for a hug, careful not to mess with her hair and makeup. "It's total insanity, but I'm proud of you for going after what you want."

"Don't be proud yet. We don't even know if this worked. This might end with Vince selling me to a seedy businessman from Iowa. We don't really know yet, do we?"

"Speaking of, have you seen Vince yet tonight? He will be here, won't he?"

Please be here, please be here, please be here. It'd be just my luck that he has a business partner who handles the club in the evenings so he can spend his Saturday nights with some ho who isn't me.

A cough alerts us that we're not alone. It's Vince.

Hands in pockets and a smirk on his face. I don't know what he's amused about because I kept all those thoughts inside my head. My heart is another story. It's about to jump out of my chest at the sight of him. My pulse has most definitely increased with his arrival. Crushes are weird.

He's in a different shirt than before. The one earlier had barely discernible stripes while this one is a crisp, solid white. He's wearing a suit coat now too, black. It makes him look sexier than any man has a right to look. Sophisticated. Powerful. Sensual. I should get a hobby that is not cataloging every detail about Vince, but not right now. Maybe next week. Something like calligraphy or adult coloring books.

"Iowa's a very nice place," he says. "It's the ones from Maryland you want to watch out for."

Oh. He heard Lydia's comment about selling her to a seedy businessman who is not Rhys. Not that Rhys is seedy. He's not, not really. A little stupid in my opinion, but not seedy. Wait, that's unkind. I know he's book-smart, just love-stupid. But it's fine because Lydia is gonna fix him right up.

"Haha, you kidder, you." Lydia deflects, clearly uncomfortable that he overheard her and still a bit unsure about this entire setup.

"I'm serious," he responds, his gaze landing on mine. "As a skydiver."

Oh, my God. He remembered our conversation from earlier. I wonder if he thought about me today while I was thinking about him? Swoon. I've got the swoons. There is definitely chemistry happening here between us. A pull. A delicious gravitational force at work.

I wet my lips while I steady myself, then I smile. "Yeah, that was a good one. Skydiving safety is no joke."

Vince dips his head towards me in acknowledgment, the hint of a smirk on his face before he turns back to Lydia. "It worked," he tells her. "Rhys is here."

Lydia leaves with Vince, off to scam the love of her life into purchasing her and taking her home for sex. Scam might be too harsh a word, it's for his own good. It's an awful lot of work to go through to get laid, that's all I know.

I plop into a chair and toss my legs over the side to get comfortable, then bite my bottom lip to keep from smiling like a lunatic. Because Vince. Is. Here. I drop my head over the other arm of the chair on a groan as I think about everything I want to do to him. Or him to me. Either, both, whatever. I have got to find out if he's available before I fall any harder.

"Everything okay?"

It's Staci. She's one of the dancers here, the one who took Lydia shopping today and helped prep her for tonight. I straighten up in the chair and smile. "Yeah, I'm fine. Just daydreaming. I mean, waiting on Lydia. She just went out." I wave a hand in the direction of the door to emphasize Lydia's departure.

"Cool," Staci replies, tossing a makeup bag onto the vanity before rooting around inside of it in search of something or other. She's in yoga pants and a t-shirt, her hair damp and combed straight, so I'm guessing she's preparing to go home versus preparing to go on stage.

"Done for the night?" I question as she squirts a dollop of moisturizer onto her fingertips before working it onto her face.

"Yup." She nods as she tosses her face cream back into her makeup bag before dumping the entire thing into her handbag. "I'm gonna Netflix and chill with myself and I cannot wait. It's been a long week." She starts to hoist her bag over her shoulder and I realize this might be my golden opportunity to get some answers on Vince.

"Hey, can I ask you something?"

"Sure." She nods distractedly as she rests her weight on one hip, freeing her cell phone from her bag as she turns to look at me.

"What do you know about Vince?"

"Vince?" She seems a bit caught off guard, as if she wasn't expecting this line of questioning from me. "I mean, he's my boss?" She ends the sentence as a question, as if she has no idea what information I'm seeking. I'm not sure how that's possible, because look at him.

"Is he with anyone?"

"Ah." She smiles now, looking me over with new interest. "I don't think so."

"How is that possible?"

"I don't know." She laughs. "I think he works a lot. He's kinda serious, don't you think?" She shrugs like she hasn't given any thought to this.

"So he's not with any of the girls?" I press. I really need to know what I'm up against tonight. "Casually?"

"No, definitely not. It's kind of an unspoken rule around here. Vince doesn't cross those boundaries."

What I'm hearing is the coast is clear for me to cross some boundaries with Vince. He's becoming more and more interesting to me by the second.

"I don't think he's been with anyone seriously since Gwen," she adds, throwing me. Was Gwen a dancer who broke his heart? Did she run off with a customer? Break an ankle while wearing a stripper heel and retire to Arizona and force him to implement his no-fraternization policy with the dancers? Or did Gwen have nothing to do with the club? Maybe she was his high school sweetheart... and ran off with his best customer—a tech nerd who made billions when the stock for his app went public.

I really need to lock down my imagination.

I'm about to ask for clarity on this Gwen character when Staci's phone rings. She accepts the call while giving me her apologies about having to run. I grab a cluster of grapes and resume my position relaxing in the chair, popping grapes into my mouth while I wait. Almost as soon as Staci leaves the door swings open again and Lydia appears, collapsing against the door the moment it's swung shut again.

She's wearing a man's suit jacket over the negligée she went out there in and I don't think it would take an astrophysicist to figure out that it's Rhys' jacket. Not that there's an astrophysicist hanging around to weigh in on the topic. Or maybe there is, what do I know? There may very well be an entire group of astrophysicists hanging out downstairs. Maybe astrophysics is a field filled with kinky fuckers, but my money is on virgins living with their mothers. I've been known to be wrong a time or ten though, so don't take my word on it.

"Nice jacket," I greet her before popping another grape into my mouth.

"Payton." She braces against the door and kicks the heels on her feet off one at a time. They clatter across the floor with a thunk as she exhales. "That was horrible."

47

"What happened?" I sit up, bracing myself for something awful, but to be honest, my money is still on that being Rhys' jacket. Because he couldn't stand to see her in public wearing something less revealing than a swimsuit, so he covered her up in some kind of caveman gesture. *You woman. Me man. Mine. Grunt.*

I sorta love that kind of bullshit. It's cute.

"Lawson is out there. And Canon!"

"Oh." I lean back in the chair and get comfortable. "Well, yeah. They're friends, so that makes sense. Besides, Vince had to get Rhys here tonight. I'm sure he recruited Lawson or Canon to help him make that happen."

"Why didn't it occur to me that they might be here? I'm so embarrassed." She wraps Rhys' jacket tighter around her body and worries her bottom lip between her teeth.

"So did Rhys win you or what?"

"I don't know."

"How can you not know? That was literally the point of the auction."

"Because I don't know. One minute I was standing on stage under a spotlight and the next he was wrapping me in his jacket and telling me to get dressed." She turns around to slip the negligée off and quickly dress.

"Sounds like you're leaving with Rhys."

They're going to have really attractive babies. Lydia will make homemade organic baby food that she freezes into tiny baby-sized portions in a vintage ice cube tray she bought at the Goodwill while Rhys stares at her with a mixture of befuddlement and worship for the rest of his life. I'll babysit on occasion, take the kids out for non-organic ice cream covered in candy and then return them on a sugar high covered in streaks of chocolate and crumbs.

I'll need to borrow one of their cars for those outings, obviously.

Lydia's carefully folding Rhys' jacket when the door opens. It's Vince. Vince with an actual smile on this face. He's got his hands in his pockets, thumbs hooked on the exterior. His body language is relaxed, polar opposite to Lydia's entrance a few minutes before. His eyes rest on mine for a moment before he turns his attention to Lydia. He has curious eyes, that's how I'd describe them. There's a speck of interest when he looks at me. Amused interest, but it bodes well for me. Of course I might be projecting based on what I want to see. As long as I'm projecting I'm going to note that he looks well rested too. Like he could stay up all night if needed.

"After a small bidding war we came to an agreement at five," Vince tells Lydia.

"Got who to five?" Lydia asks, a look of confusion on her face as if she's already forgotten why she's here.

"Rhys," Vince says, looking at her like she's crazy. "Wasn't that the entire point, Lydia?"

Exactly! That's exactly what I just said! Vince and I are so in sync. God, tonight is going to be amazing.

Lydia drops into the chair next to mine and proceeds to argue with Vince about how much Rhys should have paid for her. It seems Vince thought he was being generous for not antagonizing Rhys into paying a million and Lydia thought Rhys was going to check out with a Groupon deal.

My life has gotten exponentially more entertaining since moving in with Lydia. I didn't really see that coming, to be honest. She's a bit on the quiet, goody-two-shoes side. When she's not selling her virginity to her boss, that is.

"Does he think he's getting a party?" Lydia is questioning Vince when I tune back in to their conversation. I was distracted cataloging every detail of how he looks in that suit. Is liking the way a jacket fits his shoulders a weird thing? Because I'm deeply into it. "I'm not doing his friends or anything weird like that. I'm not." She's firm about this, it would seem.

"I would," I chime in. "You only live once, am I right?"

Vince pauses at that, side-eyeing the hell out of me before running a hand over his jaw and exhaling. "I've got no idea what the guy is into," he replies, addressing Lydia. "I'm sure the two of you can figure that out. Alone. Without me," he adds in a tone tells me he's reached his limit on this charade. I can't really blame him, it's not even a real auction. It's real money, sure, but the auction was fake.

"She accepts," I announce to both of them. "You accept," I tell Lydia. "It's time to earn your Rhys badge."

"What in the hell is a Rhys badge?" Vince looks between us before shaking his head. "Never mind, I don't actually want to know. He's outside, waiting for you. It's your choice. I'm not giving him his money back though. Dumb fuck has more than he needs." He mutters the last part under his breath.

We're definitely in agreement on that. Rhys totally deserves to lose half a million dollars because Lydia would have gone home with him for free weeks ago. I love how we're already on the same page about our friends, like a team. We have so much in common it's ridiculous.

Less than five minutes later we're dropping Lydia off for her first day of school, I mean sex. We don't have kids of our own yet because it's not possible to get pregnant from eye-fucking someone.

I give Lydia a final hug as Vince holds the door open for her. I don't think Vince needed my help walking her to the door but you didn't think I was going to let him out of my sight now, did you? Lydia is not the only one getting laid tonight.

"Break a dick!" I call out to Lydia as the door swings shut behind her.

And then I'm alone with Vince.

Finally.

The sexual tension is off the charts. Way, way off.

I bet we're gonna have sex in this hallway because he won't be able to contain himself long enough to make it back to his office or to a broom closet, which is fine because I'm ready. So very ready.

He's standing so close behind me I can feel the heat and energy flaring between us without us even physically touching. I take my time turning, wanting to drag the moment out and commit it to memory forever. I wet my lips as I pivot, my eyes level with his chest. He's so appetizingly tall and broad and manly. I exhale and drag my eyes upwards, ready to tip my head back for a kiss.

Except he's laughing.

At me.

EIGHT

"IT'S 'BREAK A LEG,'" he says. "The saying. It's 'break a leg,' not 'break a dick.'"

I groan in exasperation. Now is not the time for semantics.

"Like breaking a dick wouldn't be exponentially worse?" I snap back. I can't believe this is the conversation we're having right now.

"Fair point," he says with a tip of his head, smirk still firmly in place, which annoys me enough to elaborate.

"For the record—" I hold up a finger, ready to make my case, but I'm interrupted before I can get very far.

"The record," he interrupts, his brows lifted in amusement. "Do we need a court reporter present? Should I make a call?"

Ugh, this guy.

"For the record," I start again after shooting him a look that conveys he had best let me finish, "the phrase 'break a leg' is an ironic expression of good luck. So telling someone to break a dick as they're on their way to have sex is a pretty brilliant adaption of the phrase." I cross my arms in triumph, because when you're right you're right. And I'm so right. I might even submit this phase to Urban Dictionary because I think this one has a real chance of catching on.

He laughs out loud this time before shaking his head and turning on his heel to retreat down the hallway following the path we took to get here, his footsteps reverberating on the polished concrete floors.

"You're nuts. Cute but nuts," he mutters as he starts up the stairs.

"No. I'm actually really funny. That was just proof of that." I jog up the steps so I can catch up with him at the landing and cut him off. "And no one has called me cute since I was twelve. I'm way past twelve."

"I can see that," he replies after a pregnant pause, his gaze dropping briefly to my cleavage.

Thank fuck this body shimmer is finally working.

"Good. What else do you want to see?" I rest my hand on the railing, blocking him from further escape, my head tilted to the side in what I hope appears as a blatant invitation.

"Excuse me?" He gets the most amazing line on his forehead when he narrows his eyes on me. There's a hint of a laugh on his lips warring with the flicker of disbelief in his expression and I want him to kiss me. I might die if he doesn't kiss me soon. Melt right into an angsty puddle of sexual need. Death by denial of his perfect lips.

"I'd be happy to break your dick," I offer, then wince. "Okay"—I remove my hand from the railing and hold it up in the universal stop gesture—"I'll admit that adaption didn't really work."

"Not quite." He shakes his head, a smile on his lips. I take a half a step closer to him. Damn, he smells good too. He looks good, he smells good and

I'm positive he'd taste good if I could just get his lips on mine. Or lick him. I might settle for licking him at this point if I didn't think it might make things weird.

"Whatever. You get the gist," I whisper, leaning in a bit closer. *Kiss. Me.*

"I'll pass."

Wait, what?

I'm positive if you looked up the word 'disbelief' right at this moment a picture of my face would be attached. It'd be in one of those animated three-second clips and the only thing moving on my face would be my eyelids, blinking in slow repetition.

My libido slows down a bit to give my brain a moment to catch up.

"No?" I repeat.

"Are you unfamiliar with the word, Payton?"

"You run a strip club." I'm dumbfounded. Like what the fuck?

"So you think I indiscriminately fuck anyone who offers?" He says it calmly, seemingly without any care, but his response takes a second too long and his eyes don't quite meet mine.

"No!" Sorta. Yeah, I sorta did. God, I'm awful, but really? "It's not like I thought that many women offered," I try to clarify.

His brows lift at that and then he laughs before brushing past me and continuing up the second set of steps.

"I meant outright," I protest, clambering after him. "Obviously you get plenty of offers for sex. Look at yourself, of course you do."

I'm not sure that came out right either.

"It's a very flattering offer," I add for lack of anything else to say. It really is. I'm far from hideous and besides, I'm not wrong about all the sexual tension between us. There's enough of it to power all the neon in Vegas.

We've reached the landing to the second floor and he pauses and turns to face me, his eyes dropping to my lips. Finally, finally, finally. Then he shakes his head, as if shaking sense into himself, before opening the stairwell door without a word.

This motherfucker.

"Why the hell not though?" I slide past him into the hall and stand in front of him, one hand on my hip, the other pointed in his face. "That was a great offer." I punctuate that with my finger. "Most men would be delighted with such straightforwardness."

"Would they?" The smirk is back on his stupid, perfect face. "Is it an offer you make often, Payton?"

Oh, no, he did not.

"Listen, asshole. That's really none of your business. I can hand out a golden ticket to whomever the hell I want, whenever the hell I want. The number of tickets handed out does not change my value as a female, so save your sexist bullshit for someone who cares. I'm not going to apologize for being in charge of my own sexuality and asking for what I want."

"A golden ticket. Jesus Christ, I can't with you."

"Yeah, well, I can't with you either. You're not even seeing anyone. What is your hangup?"

"I'm not seeing anyone?" He looks interested by this revelation, his brows shooting up before his lips relax into an amused grin.

"Are you?" Fuck a dildo, I should really verify my information with more than one source before I dive into things. This is exactly how I got kicked out of the Girl Troopers in the second grade. Well, not exactly.

But sorta. No, this is nothing like that.

"No," he agrees with a shrug. "I'm not."

"You are such a pain in the ass."

"So." He says it slowly as if he's in no hurry. He never speaks in a hurry though, I've noticed. I wonder if he's like this with everyone, confident enough to know that they'll wait to hear what he has to say. "I should service you on demand because I'm not otherwise involved with anyone? Is that what you're saying? Isn't that sexist as well?"

"It would be," I agree, "if you weren't every bit as attracted to me as I am to you."

"Am I?"

God, not this song and dance again.

"Yes," I insist confidently. If I'm wrong about this so help me, but I'm already in this deep, there's no point backing down now. Might as well go for broke—this is Vegas after all. Also, I've never been a coy girl. Go for the brass ring and all that. "You're curious about me," I tell him. "You look at me like I'm interesting. Or at the very least pretty."

Somewhere in this exchange he's stepped half a foot closer, but he's still not touching me.

"You like my ass," I add in a last-ditch effort because he's neither saying anything or kissing me.

He moves another inch closer and smiles. I have to tilt my head back to meet his eyes and I'm holding my breath because sexual tension is tense.

"I look at you that way because you're nuts and I never know what's about to come out of your mouth."

"Oh." Oh. I blink. Wow, did I get this wrong. My cheeks heat in embarrassment and I drop my gaze to his shoulder. I'm still really into the way the jacket fits him. Perfectly cut, the seam running from to neck to sleeve really does it for me, so there's that.

"And because you're beautiful."

Oh. Okay. We're doing a mixed signals thing. I bite my lip and risk another look at him.

"Game-changing beautiful." The words are whispered against my ear. "Possibly crazy, definitely trouble." This whispered against my lips.

And then he kisses me.

NINE

HE DOESN'T TIP my chin up with a single fingertip. No, instead he palms my jaw, his fingertips burning into the skin behind my neck, his thumb on my chin, his lips soft and firm and warm and perfectly pressed against mine. And he most certainly does not kiss me like he's indifferent to me. He kisses me like he wants to do filthy things with me.

I love it when I'm right.

It's almost as satisfying a feeling as Vince's tongue exploring my mouth, but no *I told you so* in the world could top this kiss. He tastes minty and he smells exactly like a grownup man should. Spicy and masculine. Like a forest on a fall day, with a treehouse complete with a rope ladder for climbing. He's warm, the heat of his body pleasant in a hallway I hadn't realized was chilly until I was pressed against him.

The jacket I like so much is soft gripped between my fingertips, but beneath it Vince is hard. And I don't mean his penis. If he's got a hard-on he's not grinding it against me like a randy teenager. Only a minute ago I'd have been okay with a randy teenager bump-and-grind, but not now. Now that I'm in the midst of this perfect kiss I don't want anything else. He's hard as in he's firm in all the right places. My forearms are pressed against his chest and he's so deliciously solid. The feel of him makes me feel like I'm safe. As if I've suddenly developed some kind of prehistoric appreciation for strength and virility and muscle. Or maybe it's simply an appreciation for the mental picture I've concocted of him fucking me against a wall without dropping me.

He slides his other hand into my hair and tugs, maneuvering my head to change the angle of the kiss and sending a rush of heat through me. His fingers brush against my scalp and I take back everything I said about not wanting a quick grind. I'm dying for more, anything more as long as it happens right now.

He breaks the kiss and steps back, my fingers reluctantly falling from his jacket. I'm slumped against a wall I hadn't even realized I'd been pressed against, and I'm grateful for the support. We're both breathing heavily and eyeing the other as our chests heave slightly. Somewhere a door swings shut, and a phone rings, and then it's silent.

"I told you so," I blurt out because I can't help myself. He wasted a solid five minutes playing hard to get when we could have been making out. Plus anyone who says saying *I told you so* isn't satisfying is lying. Plus plus, that kiss was even better than I imagined it, and believe me, when I imagined it it was phenomenal.

"That you did," he agrees because he's a smart man. Then he wipes his bottom lip with his thumb and I about lose my mind.

"So, your place? My place?" His place would be preferable because I already know what my place looks like and I'm nosey. "Your office?" I suggest when he doesn't say anything. "Is there a utility closet around here? I feel like you're too tall for us to have sex standing up but I'm willing to try it if you are. Unless you have a sex room with a swing or maybe a footstool."

"A sex room," he repeats slowly, head tilted slightly to the side, "with a swing."

"Okay, wow. Based on your tone I'm guessing that's a no. No need to be judgey about it." He's the one running a strip club and he's judging me for asking about a sex swing? This guy. "No worries. It's more of a bucket list item than a deal breaker."

He stares at me for a long second, blinks a couple of times, then does that head shake thing again, the one where it seems like he's trying to clear his thoughts. "It's time for you to go home," he announces, before turning on his heel and walking away. Away from me. Again.

Unbelievable. It's unbelievable because that kiss was stellar and I know he felt it too. A nun watching us through a peep hole would have felt it, for Christ's sake. Hmm, I wonder how bad it is to think about nuns while forsaking the Lord's name in the same thought? It's probably not good. A nun watching through a peep hole would have felt it too, for goodness' sake. Is that better? I don't know, the point is he's obviously got some kind of self-restraint fetish. Or he might be Catholic, same difference. Either way I need to re-evaluate my night.

Vince is headed in the opposite direction of the locker room but I follow him because I don't have any other plans and I don't want to be alone. Lydia and I have only lived together for a few weeks but I'm used to her company and the idea of going back to the apartment without her sucks. It's not that I'm incapable of being alone, but I don't prefer it. I could go to Hennigan's like Lydia assumed I was going to, but going to a bar by myself seems kinda sad. I could go back to the apartment and sit in the hot tub, but I didn't blow my hair out this afternoon just to go home and sit in a frizz bath, thank you very much. Besides, the pool closes at eleven and I had an energy drink before I left the house, so it's gonna be a long night.

Vince reaches a door and half turns, his shoulder pressed against the door as he leans in to open it. "You're still here," he points out unnecessarily, because where else would I be?

"Relax. I respect your celibate life choices. You do you." Then I breeze past him into the room because I'm not going to let his bad attitude ruin my night. I may be a girl who knows what she wants, but I also know when to quit. If he's not interested, his loss. The night is still young, there's still fun to be had.

I'm in a private room of sorts, based on the small stage and the singular pole; fewer than a dozen chairs surround the stage, which is empty. The chairs, however, are not. Two of them are occupied by a couple of executives from my workplace. Rhys' buddies. Lydia mentioned they were here and here they are. Lounging in a set of armchairs, drinks in hand, talking to a cocktail waitress. She's got her ass perched on the edge of the stage and an empty drink tray under her arm and she's laughing at something that's been said before I entered the room with Vince.

Canon Reeves and Lawson McCall. I've not actually met them but I know who they are, of course. I've seen them in passing at work but I've never had any need to interact with them, as neither works in my department. Even if they did, they're many levels farther up the food chain than me so it's not like we'd be hanging in the same meetings.

I pause mid-step, a bit unsure if meeting them for the first time in the private room of a strip club is awkward.

Definitely awkward.

For them, not me. I'm not the one paying to see tits.

"Hi, I'm Payton." I stride over and introduce myself as Vince drops into a chair beside them with a grunt.

"Lydia's friend," Canon responds, standing. "You work in event marketing."

Of course he'd know that. He's the head of security at the Windsor. Once introductions are made I sit on the edge of the small coffee table so I can face everyone. I cross my legs and lean in and not for nothing, Canon notices my tits. Too bad I'm not interested in him. The whole boss thing is really not my jam.

"The first rule of Fight Club," I start, clasping my hands together and ensuring I have everyone's attention, "is what happens at Fight Club stays at Fight Club."

"That's not the first rule of Fight Club, Payton." Vince replies drily, two fingers resting on his forehead, his arm bent resting on the arm of the chair. "You don't talk about Fight Club. You're mixing it up with 'what happens in Vegas stays in Vegas.'"

"Why can't I talk about Fight Club?" I'm indignant. "Don't start your sexist bullshit with me, Vince. I can talk about Fight Club if I want to talk about Fight Club. You are not the boss of me." Hmm, maybe the boss thing could be my jam.

"The saying, Payton. The line from the movie is 'the first rule of Fight Club is you do not talk about Fight Club.' It's not 'what happens at Fight Club stays at Fight Club.'"

"Oh. Well, I've never seen the movie." I wave a hand because the details are of little importance to me. "Besides, it's practically the same thing."

Vince stares at me. I'm pretty sure I'm less than a minute away from him kicking me out again.

"Hey, is that bourbon?" Canon is holding a glass of amber-colored liquid with one single square ice cube. "I've always wanted to try that." I pluck it out of his hand and knock it back before setting the empty glass onto the table beside me with a grimace. "Whoa, that was supposed to be sipped, wasn't it?"

"It was," Canon agrees with a grin. "But I like your style." He likes my tits too. I really should give him another thought.

"Thank you." I nod in acknowledgment of the compliment. "It's nice to be appreciated." I slide a frown over to Vince before turning my attention back to Canon again. "Do you come here often?" I bat my eyelashes at Canon in a dramatic over-the-top faux flirt.

"Why are we talking about Fight Clubs?" Vince interrupts as Canon laughs.

"Oh, right!" I drumroll my hands against my thighs for buildup. "Let's have one of those nights where we wake up tomorrow with a tiger!"

"Like *The Hangover*?" Lawson asks.

"Exactly like *The Hangover*," I agree, tapping my nose and pointing back at him with a wink and a finger gunshot.

"Yeah, I'm in," Canon agrees with an easy shrug.

"That sounds like a real great idea." This from

Vince, his tone laced with sarcasm.

Canon and I exchange an eye roll. I know it sounds like a bad idea, but my life coach said bad decisions lead to good decisions because you learn from your mistakes, and I bet this is exactly the kind of scenario she was referring to. I wonder if I can convince Vince to get a life coach.

"You've already done your good deed for the day. Let's have fun," Canon responds as I nod and order a round of shots. "Besides, it's not like you're needed here. You have a manager who runs this place."

"Is the manager hot?" I ask because hey, Vince had his chance.

"The manager is a woman," Vince retorts.

"Don't judge me," I snap back.

Canon looks between us and laughs again.

"Listen, Vince," I ask, "is it better to have loved and lost or to never have loved at all?"

"What in the hell does that even mean?" He knocks back a shot, setting the empty glass onto the coffee table with a thud before settling into his chair again. "I have no idea what expression you're fucking up this time."

"You know, I'm not sure either. I thought I was going somewhere with that but you're right, it doesn't make sense." I shrug because they can't all be winners. "The point is, we're gonna have a real good time tonight."

"Is that so?"

"Pretty sure. Or we're all getting arrested and someone will have to hold my hair while I vomit. It could go either way. It's the unknown that makes it fun, don't you think?"

Fuck it. I send the waitress back for a tray of shots. This single round bullshit isn't going to get this circus out of the bigtop. Besides, it's on Vince.

"We can skinny-dip in the fountain at the Bellagio." I start by holding up my index finger and tapping it with the opposite index finger to keep count of all the fantastic ideas I have for tonight. Which is impressive since what I had planned for tonight was having sex with Vince. Good thing I'm both adaptable and a quick thinker.

"Eh, that's not actually something we can do." This is from Canon, which hurts because I thought he was going to be my fun side piece. Wait, that's not right. I thought he was going to be my fun sidekick. Like a wingman. "Security is top-notch over there. We'd be arrested before we had a chance to get completely naked."

That's valid feedback.

"You, sir"—I point at him—"have just been promoted. Have another shot."

Shots all around.

"Okay, number one," I start over, tapping one index finger with the other again. "There's a place where we can rent fancy sports cars and drive them as fast as we want around a track. Like race car drivers!"

"They closed hours ago. And we're already tipsy so they wouldn't let us drive," Lawson points out.

God, these guys.

"Well, that's just great," I gripe. "I suppose this means that place where you can operate a bulldozer is out too."

"Probably so," Lawson agrees. "TopGolf is open."

"Oh, come on!" I toss my hands up in frustration. "I'm wearing fuck-me heels. We are not going to hit golf balls. You"—I point at Lawson—"take another shot." I scowl at all three of them. "If one of you suggests a five dollar buffet, so help me..."

Vince smiles at that. His smile is more of a smirk though, a sexy little smirk that hits me right in the gut and makes me forget that I'm over him. I stare at his lips a moment longer, remembering how they felt pressed against my own. The firmness of his chest, the soft pressure of his hand on my jaw. My heart speeds up and I lick my lips as I relive that freaking perfect kiss. So I'm not totally over him then. But really, who am I to question fate? I'm not the fate police. Plus it's been like twenty minutes. I'm not made of stone.

"Number one," I repeat for the third time, then stop myself. I need to treat this trio like I treat bridezillas: limit their choices. "Forget the numbers. We're moving to a lettered system. Your choices are A or B. Got it?"

Canon and Lawson nod. Vince winks.

"You." This time I point at Vince. "Why are you all winky and flirty and pretty and kissy? I tried to fast-pass you and you turned me down! Yet you keep looking at me, sitting there all broody and mysterious like every woman's bad boy dream come to life. Looking at me with your perfect face and your kissable lips and your panty-melting brown eyes. Doing that thing with your eyes. Like you're undressing me and liking what you see. You're driving me crazy! Just"—I wave my hand around in a gesture similar to the one I use to dry my nails—"look somewhere else."

"A fast pass?" Vince is laughing now, and he's not even attempting to honor my request to stop looking at me. Nope. Instead he's looking directly at me, his grin fading into a lazy smirk before he drags his eyes over me from head to toe and back again. Slowly.

Deliberately. Infuriatingly.

"Stop looking at me!"

He won't. He's looking at me like he like I'm fascinating, which is my kryptonite. Wait, did I ever figure out if I was using that word correctly? I don't think I did. In any case, I like it, the way he looks at me. I don't think the way he looks at me is going to cause me a slow and painful death. Definitely not.

Maybe.

Okay, it might.

"Everyone focus," I announce. "Back to your choices. Option A: we can skydive off the side of the Stratosphere, or Option B: ride the roller coaster at New York, New York."

"What's option C?" Canon asks, brows drawn together. I think he's unimpressed with my idea.

"There is no option C." I glare at Canon. "A or B. Firm and final."

TEN

OPTION C, AS IT turns out, is Fremont Street. "Old-school Vegas," Canon called it.

Whatever, it'll still be fun. Thrill rides and alcohol don't really mix anyway. We take a town car from the club. Apparently they've got them on standby because providing customers with a free ride is a thing. I told Vince if his customers didn't have the money for a cab they surely didn't have the money to pay for lap dances. He didn't think that was funny. He's wrong, but it's okay because I'm not a grudge-holder.

It's not far to Fremont, but it's Saturday night in Vegas so it takes twenty minutes to go three miles. Twenty minutes in which I'm pressed against Vince in the back seat of the town car. Twenty long, hard minutes.

For me. Who the hell knows what Vince is feeling.

I love being pressed against him. There's more than enough room in the back seat of this car for me not to be near sitting on Vince's lap, but seize the day, am I right? He's warm and soft and hard and delicious. I know that's an oxymoron, soft and hard. But he's so perfectly male. Big and firm, yet his shoulder makes such a nice place for me to rest my head.

"Are you comfortable?"

So my cuddling hasn't gone unnoticed.

"Not as comfortable as I would have been on your desk," I reply.

Beside me he snorts in response. I wonder if he's on a sex cleanse, like when people give up sugar or gluten, but a hundred times worse.

On the other side of me Canon is thumbing through his phone, ignoring us. Lawson is in the front, embroiled in a conversation about hockey with the driver. At least I think it's hockey. Irrelevant to me, that's all I know.

We stop in front of the Golden Nugget and pile out of the car. The curb is on Canon's side of the car, so I take my time, knowing Vince will have to look at my ass as I bend just so to exit. Then I pause on the pavement, smug in my seduction techniques, and give my behind a little shake as I smooth my hair over my shoulders before moving out of the way.

Except.

Except he got out on the other side and walked around and missed my entire performance. I sigh audibly as Canon turns to face me.

"Relax," he tells me. "This is better than SkyJumping, trust me."

"It's great." I force a smile because he's right. I didn't even want to SkyJump, not really. I don't want to beat a dead horse about my hair, but pretty sure jumping off the side of a building would have rendered my blowout useless.

We go inside and Canon turns to me with a grin. "A or B," he says and I smile. Then he winks and I laugh. "A, we play craps. B, we play baccarat."

"I don't know what either of those games are so let's go with A." I shrug.

It turns out that I'm pretty good at craps. Technically I understand that you can't be good at something that involves nothing but random luck, but I like to take my wins where I can and it turns out I've got a real flair for throwing sevens.

I've got a flair for having a good time too.

One tequila...

"To tigers!" I raise my glass to toast. "Bottoms up!"

Fucking tigers.

I blame the tigers for everything that happens next.

Blaming tequila would be more logical, but nothing that happens next is logical, so tigers might as well take the responsibility.

Two tequila...

"What is it you want, Payton?"

"Fun. I want to have fun."

"Maybe I'm not interested in fun." He's standing so close to me, his eyes steady on mine and his expression hard to read.

"You legiterally run a strip club. Fun is your middle name."

"Legiterally?" The corner of Vince's mouth pulls upwards and his eyes flash in amusement. Dark chocolatey brown eyes with specks of amber and honey and lust. Lust is a color, trust me.

"Yeah, it's when something is too legit to quit."

"It's not." Vince shakes his head in response, the smirk transformed into a wide smile now.

"I'm pretty sure it is," I argue, but I'm cut off because his lips are on mine. He tastes like expensive alcohol and great ideas.

Three tequila...

"We are such a good idea," I tell Vince.

"Are we?"

"The best idea ever."

"Hmm," he hums against my neck because he's sucking my earlobe into his mouth. Praise Jesus.

"You know what we could do?" I ask.

"What's that?"

"We could make out behind that pinball machine." We're in an arcade because, well, because it's here and who doesn't love an arcade? Also because option A was ziplining and none of the guys wanted to zipline.

Confession: I knew they wouldn't want to, which is why I paired it with the arcade. I have a real weakness for Skee-Ball.

"I don't think that would work."

"Why not?"

"Because the pinball machine is not an invisibility cloak and public fornication is illegal in Las Vegas."

"Oh, my God. You're a dirty talker! This is so much more than I deserve. Say fornication again."

Four...

"A or B," I announce for at least the tenth time tonight, flinging my arm wide. The foot-tall slushy I'm holding would likely slosh over the side if I hadn't already drunk half of it. Slosh, such a good word. "We still haven't found a tiger." I look up and down Fremont Street with sadness. Not a tiger in sight.

"I don't think a tiger was a reasonable goal for the night, sweets," Vince comments from beside me.

"No one gets to tell me how big my dreams can be,

Vince." I heard that advice during my life coaching session. Now seems like the perfect time to implement it.

"Fair enough," he agrees.

"I'll get one tattooed on my ass. That'll count."

"You'll do no such thing."

"I knew you liked my ass. I knew it! Just so you know, I'm not opposed to butt stuff."

"You mentioned that an hour ago."

"I did? Oh."

"What's the B, Payton?" Vince smirks like he's so smart. Like a simple A or B option is going to lure me away from my tiger goal. "If A is you getting a tiger tattooed on your ass, what's option B?"

"Getting married." God, he thinks he's so smart— well, take that, Mr. Smarty Pants.

"Seems like a clear choice then, doesn't it?"

"Uh-huh." I think I'll get something tasteful, like a tiger holding a shot glass. Something to remember the night by.

"B it is."

You know what they say about Vegas, right? Don't ask, don't tell?

Just kidding.

I'm going to tell you everything.

Just give me a moment. And an aspirin.

ELEVEN

OH, GOD.

Okay, give me a second. I've got this—of course I do. I'm not an amateur for crying out loud, I can hold my liquor. By which I mean I wasn't that drunk. By which I mean I didn't black out. By which I mean I remember enough to know exactly how I ended up in the honeymoon suite of the Windsor hotel.

The details might be a little fuzzy, sure. But fuzzy doesn't mean you don't remember, it just means the details made more sense as they were happening than they make the next day, that's all.

I'm married. To Vince. That part would be crystal clear even if there wasn't a shiny gold band on my finger to remind me. I remember most of it, in a fuzzy way. I'm positive it made more sense last night, but tequila will do that to you.

Canon was my maid of honor. That part is a bit hazy, but I do remember him yelling "Shotgun, maid of honor!" as if he was calling dibs on sitting in the front seat of a car. Then he put himself in charge of the photos and insisted on comping us a stay in this honeymoon suite. And he was really into that something old, something new, something borrowed, something blue bullshit, but I can't quite remember the details.

Wait, it's the suite. He said it was new because no one had actually stayed in it yet. And borrowed because he was comping it. He said the something old was Vince. What in the hell was the something blue though? Wait—it's the shower. All the suites in this hotel have blue tile in the bathrooms. I groan as softly as possible in order not to wake Vince as I slap a hand over my eyes.

That freaking shower. I don't think I'll be able to shower again without being turned on. Ever. I'll probably have to allocate time to rubbing one out every time I take a shower for the rest of my life, as I've now been conditioned to equating showering with seeing Vince naked. Naked and wet and sudsy and generous with his tongue.

By generous I mean talented and possibly in possession of magical abilities.

Scientists will tell you that it takes twenty-one days to form a habit, but no scientist has ever had Vince's tongue on their clit so I don't think they have a clue about how fast habits can form, because oh, sweet holy Jesus, trust me when I tell you that you'd only need one night with Vince's tongue to want it habitually. Though now that I think about it I learned that twenty-one days thing from a Facebook post so it's likely not even true. Vince's tongue is verified true, I can promise you that.

It was a really great night.

A perfect night.

Best night ever.

I need to hold onto those memories because when he wakes up he's going to kill me. And honestly? I can't face it. Not yet. Not after the way he looked at me last night, like marrying me was the best decision of his life. Last night he made me believe in love at first sight and fairy tales and happily ever afters and forever. Though it could have been the tequila making me believe, if I'm being fair. In any case, I don't think he's going to wake up today and ask me to meet his mother. On a scale of one to ten I'd say the likelihood of that happening is a one.

He's going to wake up and look at me like I'm a drunken mistake. And then demand that we get this dissolved as quickly as possible.

Which I get, I do. I've known him a day, it's not like we're in love or anything. That would be silly. Not totally unheard of, it does happen. In movies mostly, but sometimes it happens to your friend's cousin's next-door neighbor. So it could. But it hasn't happened here, because only one of us is crazy.

Unless.

Unless he was so blown away with what a good time I am that he decided he best put a ring on it? Doubtful, but possible. I am a real good catch. I have a college degree, and a job. A job with benefits! I wonder if he needs health insurance? I could add him to my health plan at work now that we're married. Then I'd be a wife with benefits, which is way better than a friend with benefits because he'd get affordable healthcare and sex.

But that's likely not a selling point, mostly because I'm betting he has health insurance already. He seems like he has his act together, aside from marrying me last night, obviously.

In any case, I can't face him this morning. I can't do it. I know I'll have to do it eventually, but today is not that day. Don't I deserve just one day? One day to revel in the memories of the best night of my life? One day to pretend whirlwind romances exist?

One day to believe in love.

One day to pretend it exists.

That sounds fair.

Fair-ish.

Fair if we're grading on a bell curve where one of us gets what they want and the other doesn't. Wait, is that a bell curve? No, I don't think I'm using that correctly at all.

I take one last look at him before I get out of bed. He's on his back, one hand resting on his stomach and the other on my shoulder, because I'm snuggled into the side of him like a needy kitten. He's wearing a gold band on the third finger of his left hand, the hand resting on his stomach. His perfectly chiseled six-pack of a stomach. He's got that V thing too—you know those abdominal muscles that make women stupid? He's got 'em. And they lead directly to the holy grail of penises. My vagina throbs just glancing at it. Literally. Throbbing in denial because all I got penetrated with last night was his tongue and a finger, so I need to get out of this bed right now before I do something stupider than marrying him. Something like waking him up with a demand to ride his cock only to have the moment ruined when he remembers he lost his ever-loving mind last night by marrying a crazy girl.

One more moment of lustful staring will have to do. It's just, is there anything hotter than a wedding band on the finger of a very sexy man? Like, look at that sexy motherfucker committed to fucking only one woman for the rest of his life. Rawr. Is it just me? It can't be just me.

And seeing a ring on a man that belongs to you?

Whole new level of hot.

Even if it's temporary.

Maybe I'll take a quick picture of it. The sheet is

covering his junk so it's not totally invasive taking his picture while he's asleep, right? Not more invasive than marrying him while he was drunk.

Or did he marry me while I was drunk?

Hmm?

We were both drinking, we're both to blame. That's not even me rationalizing, it's true. It's still a mess though. A big ole hot mess. One that I'd prefer to deal with tomorrow, so right now, I need to go. I ease out of his arms and slip out of the bed, tossing a regretful glance back at Vince as I go.

He has nice lips too. I don't think I've given enough credit to those lips because I've been sidetracked over his tongue. But his lips. Hmm. Full, soft, good at sucking.

Focus, Payton.

I find my phone and notice that I already have a picture of Vince wearing his wedding ring. I notice it because I've made said picture the screensaver on my phone.

At least my drunk self and my sober self are consistent.

Consistently nuts.

Wouldn't it be great if my drunk self was some kind of secret genius who did difficult things like making sound financial investments instead of easy things like picking a good photo of Vince? Drunk Payton did pick a good photo though, I gotta give her credit for that.

My camera roll is jam-packed with selfies from last night. On Fremont Street. At the chapel. In bed. Some are of Vince alone. Sometimes he's smiling. Sometimes he's brooding. Sometimes he has no idea his picture is being taken. But most of them are of us together. Smiling, laughing, me making ridiculous faces while Vince makes a normal face.

Us. I exhale hard. *Us is not a thing, Payton.*

TWELVE

AFTER COLLECTING MY clothing from around the hotel suite I quietly get dressed and then slip out, fuck-me heels dangling from my fingertips and a stuffed shark shoved under my arm until I reach the hallway, easing the suite door closed behind me and slipping the heels onto my feet. Vince won the shark for me last night at the arcade and I have big plans to sleep with it until I'm forty.

I say a silent thank you to Jesus for making today a Sunday because it means I get to do the walk of shame through the hotel—the same hotel I work at—while bumping into as few co-workers as possible.

I left my car at home last night because I'd intended to ride Vince's dick home from Double Diamonds, so I order an Uber in the elevator. Then I hold my head up high and glide straight through the lobby to the cab pickup line, waving hello to Henry in bellhop services and Renee working the concierge desk. Fuck 'em. This could be my church outfit, they don't get to judge me.

Still, I breath a sigh of relief once I'm in the Uber. God, last night was fun. The most fun I've ever had. Obviously I'd left the house intent on having a good time, but you can't plan a night like that. You can't plan to laugh so hard you have to squeeze your legs together so you don't pee. You can't plan on tripping and nearly running into an Elvis impersonator riding a bicycle with a parrot on his shoulder, then getting pulled back in the nick of time by Vince as he says, "To hell with it," and kisses you until you're so breathless you're not sure if it's from your near-death experience or from his lips. You can't plan on the slushies being available in foot-long penis-shaped containers. That's just good luck.

You can't know that stopping for a slice of pizza will result in triggering a memory of that Halloween party in college where you thought a raccoon was a cat. So you left the door of the frat house open for him, thinking how great it was that these guys had a frat-cat. But then the frat-cat nabbed a slice of pizza right out of the box and everyone flipped the fuck out because it was a frat-coon, not a frat-cat. The term 'frat-coon' makes everyone laugh even more than it did when you coined it the first time.

"I love how you make him laugh," Canon says. I know he means Vince because we lost Lawson somewhere in the last round of drinks. It's hard to keep track when you're drinking. I think that saying is supposed to be about fun, not people, but honestly if you think about it it totally applies to people. They are really hard to keep track of in Vegas.

"How is he laughing though? Is it like 'haha, I want to bang you' or 'haha, I think you're a clown?'"

"He doesn't think you're a clown."

"Canon Reeves, you are the best wingman ever."

"That"—he points his beer at me—*"is a fact. I really don't get enough credit for it."*

You can't know that Vince Rossi actually is a filthy dirty talker way, way, way out of your dirty-talking league and is in fact your kryptonite no matter what that word means. He's it. All of it. Everything.

"I need you, Vince."

"Do you? Is your pussy wet for me, Payton? Wet and needy and hungry for my cock?"

"It is, actually."

"Maybe I'll give it to you later."

"Please." I lean closer, breathing the word onto him. He is such a fucking tease.

"I like it when you beg."

"Jesus. I'll crawl on the floor and take off your belt with my teeth if that's what you're into." That's partially a lie. I have no idea how to undo a belt with my teeth.

"I'd rather see you face down on my bed, ass in the air with my come dripping down your thighs."

Oh. Holy. Shit. Hollleeee shit.

"That would be fine," I finally manage to agree as nonchalantly as possible.

"It'd be better than fine, I can promise you that."

You can't know that suggesting A, you get a tiger tattooed on your ass or B, you get married would result in ending the night with a husband. I mean I knew he liked my ass. Liked it so much he'd be willing to marry me to stop me from defiling it with a tiger tattoo? I had no idea.

"I Payton, take you, Vince, to be my lawfully wedded husband. Before these witnesses, I promise never to get a tiger tattooed onto my ass. Never, ever."
"And?" Vince prompts.
Oh, yeah. *"I vow that I have handed out my last golden ticket. Till death do us part."*

If I could have planned all of that I'd be the event planner of the century. That was more of an adrenaline-fueled, hormone-boosted, alcohol-driven happenstance.

Except that 'happenstance' is just another word for 'coincidence.' And we all know that 'coincidence' is simply a boring word for 'fate,' so maybe none of this is my fault. I'd be fine with that explanation, because I'm a reasonable person, but I don't know enough about my new husband to know if he'll agree.

My husband. Husband. It's such a good word, isn't it? Maybe this is why my mother has gotten married so many times? Maybe this is one of those things I can only appreciate about her as an adult? I mull it over for a second and decide it's not and I don't.

Then I'm home, the Uber coming to a stop in front of my apartment building so I can stop dwelling on stupid shit and start thinking about the real issues I'm facing. Namely, if I'm out of Cheez-Its or not. But it turns out I've got bigger issues because when I unlock my door I find Rhys standing in my kitchen.

Oh, Jesus Christ. Rhys and Lydia. I forgot all about Lydia losing her virginity while I was sidetracked getting married. I am the worst friend in the world. Also, I've not actually met Rhys before so this is awkward. Again, for him, not me. I'm not the one who can't get off without paying for it. But still, you'd think I could meet one of these guys in a normal way.

Lydia emerges from her bedroom and introduces us, then gives me a second glance. "Payton, why are you still wearing the same thing you had on last night?" Sweet clueless Lydia. Also, fuck my life, I cannot catch a break today.

"Am I? Enough about me. How was the sex last night?" Partly that's a deflection, partly I really want to know. I gave away my virginity in high school to a guy who probably still thinks it was the best lay of my life. It wasn't.

"Payton!" Lydia is mortified. "I'm not going to tell you what Rhys is like in bed when he's standing right here."

That's fair. If by that she means she's going to tell me about it later. If not, it's bullshit.

"So what are you guys doing today?" I glance between her and Rhys, confused about why he's in our apartment. I assume he's dropping her off from their night of debauchery but I don't know why he's still here.

"I'm just packing a few things," Lydia says, heading back to her room. "Rhys wants me to stay over for a while."

Oh, right, that month-long thing. I was kinda hoping we were going to ease into this by splitting Lydia like one splits a child during a custody arrangement. He'd get her on Wednesday evenings and every other weekend and I'd get her the rest of the time. I feel a lump in my throat, realizing that this is it. She's packing up to spend the month with him, which means I'm never getting her back. She's going to move in with him and make him crockpot dinners and sew buttons back on his shirts like it's 1957 and he's going to fall in love with her and keep her in his ivory tower with him forever.

"I live in a hotel, not in a castle," Rhys responds, looking at me like I'm nuts, and I realize I might have said part of that aloud. Sue me, it's been a long night and I'm dehydrated.

THIRTEEN

ONCE RHYS AND Lydia leave I find a box of Cheez-Its and a bottle of Gatorade and take them into the shower with me. What? Like you've never eaten crackers in the shower after a rough night? I'm just a girl trying her hardest, don't judge me. Besides, the countertop in my bathroom runs right up to the shower, so technically the crackers weren't *in* the shower.

'Technically' is a word people use when they want to draw murky lines around their behavior and deflect away from information they might regret providing you with.

I've toweled off and am halfway into a pair of yoga pants when my phone starts buzzing with incoming texts. Texts from Canon, oddly. Odd because I don't have Canon's phone number and I've never added him to my phone as a contact. Yet here he is.

Canon Reeves: Vince is looking for you

Canon Reeves: How was the honeymoon suite?

Canon Reeves: Make sure you leave a nice review online. It's the least you can do

Canon Reeves: A review about the suite, not Vince. That kind of language will get the review bounced

Me: HOW ARE YOU PROGRAMMED INTO MY PHONE AND HOW DO YOU HAVE MY PHONE NUMBER?

Canon Reeves: Oh, that was easy.

Me: Really?

Canon Reeves: Yeah. I pulled your number from your employment file. Then I hacked into your phone and added myself as a contact so my texts would show up with my name so you'd answer them. You're welcome.

Me: REALLY?

Canon Reeves: Yeah, like I said, it's not that hard.

Me: Not what I meant by REALLY, dick. INAPPROPRIATE use of my personal information.

Canon Reeves: Oh. So you didn't want a heads-up that Vince is on his way?

Me: His way where?

Canon Reeves: To your apartment.

Me: How does he know I'm at my apartment...

Canon Reeves: Location services on your phone. It's easy.

Me: OMG.

Canon Reeves: No, really. A child could track you this way.

Me: NOT WHAT I MEANT.

Canon Reeves: Should I add Vince's number to your contacts? I was going to do it but I wasn't sure how to enter his info. Vince Rossi? Husband? Boo? BAE?

Me: ...

Canon Reeves: ...

Me: So you hacked me, stalked me and gave Vince my address?

Canon Reeves: He knows I know how to do it. What was I gonna do, tell him no?

Me: Yes?

Canon Reeves: Don't put me in the middle, bro. He's my friend but I feel some loyalty to you after you made me your maid of honor last night.

Me: Not exactly how I remember it...

Canon Reeves: I picked out your goddamned veil. Just let me have my moment for fuck's sake.

I'm about to reply when the banging on my front door starts. The banging is overkill because these apartments have doorbells. It's Vince, obviously. Unless I've entered an episode of a murder mystery program and a serial killer has selected this moment to randomly knock on my door.

Peephole confirmation: it's Vince.

Canon sucks at giving a heads-up. My hair is still damp while Vince has clearly had time to shower, shave and drive over here. And he's not in last night's clothing either, so he's been home. He looks good. I bet he didn't take a shower with crackers.

The knocking stops and he gives the peephole a dirty look before he speaks in a volume that makes me think he knows I'm standing on the other side of the door. "I know you're home, Payton. Open the door."

I sigh. Maybe this won't be so bad. Maybe he needs health insurance or a wife for an inheritance, you never know.

I open the door.

He's braced one arm on the doorframe, his body filling the entire space. He looks even better today than he did last night, which should be impossible but is unfair if nothing else. He runs his gaze over me. I'm wearing a faded LSU t-shirt and yoga pants. My hair is still damp and I'm not wearing a drop of makeup. He looks like a god in a fresh-pressed shirt, sleeves rolled to the elbow, and a pair of worn-in jeans. Neither of us says anything.

"We should talk." He finally speaks after it's clear I'm not going to. He's still standing in my doorway because I've not moved out of the way or invited him in either.

"Or we should have tacos?" I offer just in case the A or B game is still in effect. Talking versus tacos would be an easy pick for me.

He lifts his hand. He's holding an iced coffee and a Del Taco bag. Holy crap. How did he know I wanted tacos before I told him I wanted tacos? He really is my one true love.

"How did you know I wanted tacos?" I ask, stepping back to allow him inside because show me a girl who doesn't open the door for tacos and I'll show you a grasshopper. I know that made no sense, but really, what would have? Show me a girl who doesn't like tacos and I'll show you... what? That idiom was destined to fail from the start. Anyway, I let him in because we've got that whole married thing going on so it seems like it would be rude to make him eat tacos on my doorstep.

"You mentioned it fifteen times last night."

"I did?" God, what else did I mention? I'm fairly proud of my memory retention but I don't recall anything about tacos.

"You did. Right before you told us the frat-coon story you said that you should never have given us the choice between A, tacos and B, pizza because you really wanted tacos."

"Oh." I tap my lip with my finger. That does sounds accurate. Nothing against pizza, I just really really wanted a taco.

"Then you sang about tacos during karaoke."

"Stop it. That did not happen." I walk the ten feet

to the kitchen table, Vince right behind me.

"'I love tacos,'" Vince starts in a voice that is clearly meant to be mine as he sets the takeout bag on the table. "'I love tacos for lunch or dinner. Beef or chicken, it doesn't matter.'"

Wait. That sounds familiar…

"'I love them with lettuce and shredded cheese, jalapeños on the side or they'll be denied.'"

Oh, God. I was rhyming. Goddamn tequila.

"'Soft or crunchy, they're always yummy.'"

"Okay, stop!" I think I'm blushing. The man has seen my vagina up close and personal and I'm blushing over a taco song. Oh, the irony. "Maybe that happened." I drop into a seat without looking at him. He sets the iced coffee down on the table in front of me before unpacking the tacos. The straw is already in the cup with two inches of wrapper left on the end like a tiny straw condom. I take it off and stick it in my mouth—the straw, not the wrapper. I glance up at him while I suck and imagine what having Vince in my mouth would feel like. Vince's eyes darken as he watches me slide the straw between my lips and I think we might have matching visualization boards right now.

It occurs to me that I'm the worst wedding night lay in the history of wedding nights. I lost count of how many times he got me off and I didn't even give him a blow job. I did give him a hand job in the shower so at least there's that.

I take another drag on my iced coffee while I sulk. I always imagined myself as a very generous wife, sexually. It was how I was going to compensate for having no interest in crockpots or any desire to pick up dry cleaning.

He clears his throat as he pulls two bottles of

water out of the bottom of the bag and sets one in front of me.

"You should hydrate," he instructs as he pulls out the chair beside mine.

"I had a Gatorade in the shower." Now that I think of it, I think I lost some time in the shower because I'm not sure where this morning has gone. Wait—I know what happened. I was masturbating to the memory of the shower I had with Vince last night. Son of a bitch, I'm going to have to start getting up early for work now.

"That sounds about right," Vince murmurs, uncapping his water and tipping it back to his lips. Do not look at his lips, do not look at his lips, do not look at his lips. I grab a taco and unwrap it, then take a bite and examine the wrapper while I chew. Shredded cheese is delicious.

Also, I'm an idiot.

I'm having tacos with a total stranger who just happens to be my husband because I'm a complete idiot. A hot mess. A disaster of epic proportions.

I've fucked up royally.

I take another bite because really, this taco is all I have going for me right now. It's a crunchy taco and Vince isn't speaking so the soundtrack for the entire apartment is nothing but me crunching and I don't even care. I keep my head down and take another bite.

Vince unwraps a taco and I notice he's still wearing his wedding ring, as am I. It didn't even occur to me to take mine off. I should though, shouldn't I? I can't very well wear it to work this week, unless maybe I stack a few rings around it and pretend it doesn't mean anything? Like it's just part of a fun set of rings I picked up along with a husband over the weekend.

God. I'm a mess. Keeping the ring on will not make any of this more real. I'm the worst first date in the history of first dates. Like a first-date praying mantis. The fact that we weren't even on a date is not lost on me. I've got skills, man. Terrible, terrible skills.

I manage to consume three tacos and take a drag on my iced coffee, rattling the ice around the cup as I do before Vince speaks. I've been staring at the table and cramming tacos in my face so I've not given him much of an in conversationally. He's eaten two tacos. They were both soft shell with chicken. I made a note of it so that I'll have a few facts to remember him by. Likes soft-shell tacos, is good at arcade games, likes Scotch, is good at eating my pussy, likes poker.

"So we should talk," Vince prompts.

"Or we should have sex," I counter-offer, because I like both tacos and sex. It's a good offer. Generous even. I'm a giver.

"Why is that?"

Oh, God, maybe he's the idiot? "Because it's fun," I reply in the most duh tone of voice I can summon. "And because your tongue is amazing," I add before thinking better of it. Not because I'm above giving him a compliment, but because it just doesn't seem like the time for it.

Vince takes a slow pull on his bottle of water, eyes on mine as he tips it back and drinks. When he's through, he wets his lips with his tongue and I'm not sure if it's intentional, but it's effective all the same.

"You're very demanding," he notes. Okay, so he's not totally unobservant.

I shrug.

"So how do you see this playing out?" He says it casually in that calm, unhurried way he has about him. I've got no idea if he means our marriage or my request to have sex, so I go with the one I'm more interested in discussing.

"Missionary, actually. But not boring, so maybe my hands are pinned above my head or one of my knees is hiked over your shoulder so you can get in really deep. I was picturing it a little rough, a good hard fuck with me flat on my back. But whatever you like, I'm flexible. Legiterally."

Vince rubs a thumb across his bottom lip, his eyes on mine. He's got the hottest beard. The hair is short, more like a thick stubble, but dark and I find it sexy as all hell. I also think it might have given him an unfair advantage in the oral department, but then again I'm the one who benefited, so if his stubble brushing against my bare pussy gives him a head start who am I to complain? I'm not the oral Olympics judge.

Vince stands and pushes his chair in. There are still half a dozen uneaten tacos piled on the table between us as he leans down, bracing his weight on his knuckles as he bends closer. Then he pauses, and for a moment I'm unsure if he's going to say anything or just push back and leave.

"Stand up."

I push my chair back from the table and stand, the scrape of wood against tile doing little to calm my nerves. Nerves because I'm not exactly sure where this is going but I'm hoping it's going exactly where I want it to go. By it I mean Vince's penis inside my vagina. He's been a real dick tease thus far.

He signals with his hand for me to walk, his eyes

flickering between the two open bedroom doors off the living room. I swallow and walk towards mine, feeling him directly behind me. I stop when I've reached the side of my bed. Vince has stopped in the doorway of my bedroom.

"My roommate isn't coming home," I offer. "She stopped by earlier to pick up some of her stuff and then left with Rhys."

Vince nods but doesn't speak, hands in his pockets as he leans against the doorframe while he visually inspects my bedroom. I don't feel like there's that much to see since I only moved in a few weeks ago. A queen-sized bed with an upholstered headboard, a dresser and a matching nightstand. But he seems to find it all very interesting, based on his slow perusal. The lamp, the mini-blinds, the tank top hanging from the knob on my closet door—his gaze covers it all, slowly, methodically. A smiles tugs at his lips when he sees the shark from last night on my pillow.

When his eyes move back to mine his brows rise, as if he's confused about why I'm standing there watching him.

"Undress."

I lift my shirt over my head before dragging the yoga pants down my legs, kicking them free of my ankles then snaking a hand behind my back to unclip my bra. I'm not particularly graceful or seductive, but I'm wearing a t-shirt and yoga pants so I don't think there's any way around that. Vince watches as my bra falls free, the straps sliding down my arms before it drops to the floor. His eyes trail downwards to the cotton boy shorts covering my bottom and he wets his lips with his tongue as I shimmy out of those too.

He steps towards me, one step, two. When he's standing directly before me he takes my face in both hands and kisses me. It's soft and unhurried and perfect, his head dipped to reach my lips, me raised on my tiptoes to meet his. I'm pressed along the length of him, my hands gripping his forearms for leverage. The brush of his clothing along my naked skin reminds me that he's still fully dressed while I'm naked and needy and ready. It's delicious, the feeling of being exposed to him. My heart races as his lips press against mine, his tongue sliding between them, exploring my mouth as his thumbs caress my cheekbones. The stubble on his skin scratches mine, the slight abrasion some kind of direct line to my clit.

It's good.

It's every bit as good as I remember from last night, which is impossible because it's also better than I remember. Better than any kiss ever.

Then he's stepping back, the kiss broken as he moves away, his thumb swiping at his bottom lip as he does. I lick mine in response.

"On the bed," he instructs. "Flat on your back." He says it in a tone that tells me he's reminding me that this is how I asked for it. It's a bit sarcastic but he's eyeing me with nothing like sarcasm so I crawl onto the bed and position myself in the center before lying back and watching him. He's watching me like he's got all the time in the world. It makes me feel filthy to be naked while he's dressed. A good kind of filthy, like I belong to him to do with as he pleases. I find I like that. I like it very much.

His hands move to the buttons on his shirt, making slow work of slipping them free.

"Spread your legs."

I swallow hard as I move my legs apart. My heart is racing and I pray to the sweet sex goddess Aphrodite that this is really happening and that he doesn't have a sadistic plan to make me masturbate in front of him while he watches, fun as that sounds.

"Condoms?" he asks with a glance at my nightstand.

Thank you, Aphrodite, Eros, Himeros and Pothos. Thank you, PornHub and—wait. He didn't bring his own?

"Is that why we didn't have sex last night? You didn't have a condom? For fuck's sake. I had twelve in my handbag. We really need to learn how to communicate better." I use my toe to point towards the small clutch I was using last night, now lying on my dresser.

"Twelve, huh?" He abandons unbuttoning his shirt and picks up my handbag.

"I had a lot of faith in your stamina, okay? It's a compliment."

"So you left the house last night intending to sleep with me?"

"I left your office yesterday afternoon intending to sleep with you. I spent all afternoon primping and picking out an outfit that made my butt look good." He doesn't need to know I've been visualizing his sexual prowess since I saw him in the lobby of the Windsor earlier this week. A girl has to have some secrets. Plus it makes me sound like a nyphomaniac and I'm not, really. More of a situational nympho. The situation being Vince.

"Hmm," he murmurs in response to that, but his eyes trail slowly over me from head to toe before he turns his attention back to my handbag. He's cataloging my handbag with the same interest he did my bedroom, which is fine because there's not much in there, and besides, I'm naked so I don't think anything he finds is going to embarrass me right now.

"Chapstick, lipstick, hair thingy." He lays them out on my dresser one by one. "Condoms," he announces, pulling them from my bag like a gaggle of clowns piling out of a tiny car. They're still in one long strip, each one attached to the next. He removes them slowly, so that they unfold one by one, until an eighteen-inch-long strip of condoms is dangling from his fingertips once he's pulled them free of my bag.

Okay, seeing it like this twelve might have been ambitious, or a poor use of space planning for such a small bag. Like when people who buy tiny houses insist they need space for forty-seven coffee mugs. Five would be sufficient in both cases.

He rips one off the end and tosses it onto the bed before dropping the remaining eleven onto my dresser.

"An individual packet of lube?" Vince holds that up, brows raised in interest, a smirk pulling at his lips before he tosses it onto the dresser. "You don't have any issues with lubrication."

Oh, God. Okay maybe I was wrong about the potential for embarrassment.

"It was a free sample," I offer. Is it me or is he taking forever to riffle through my things and take off his pants? "It came with the box of condoms."

"Hmm." He hums again then goes back to rooting through my bag. "A travel toothbrush and two packets of single-use toothpaste." Yeah, it isn't me. He's taking forever. Also, how much more shit did I cram in that bag? It's barely big enough to hold a sandwich. Fuck's sake. I wiggle my toes and exhale, trying to be patient.

"Another hair thingy. Forty dollars in cash, a Tennessee driver's license and a credit card." He pauses and I hope that's the end of my handbag inventory. "Are you planning on staying?"

"I haven't moved!" I protest, thumping one of my spread feet against the mattress.

"Staying in Nevada," he clarifies, amused. "You have thirty days to change your license and register your vehicle with the state. The fine for not registering your car is a thousand dollars."

I married a goody-two-shoed strip club owner. What are the odds?

"You know, your foreplay chit-chat could use some improvement."

"Duly noted."

"I'm saying it as a favor. A little dirty talk not centered around the contents of a girl's handbag wouldn't kill you. The tacos were a nice touch though. Don't lose the tacos in your seduction line-up."

"Payton." He says it like a question, so I respond when he doesn't elaborate further.

"Yes?"

"Roll over. Ass up, elbows on the mattress." His hands have moved to his belt, the buckle clanking as he frees the strap, and I'm caught off guard, unsure what is happening. "Now."

FOURTEEN

"ARE YOU GOING TO spank me?" I throw a cautious look at him as I move to turn over. I don't particularly mind if he does. I'd just like to know. Or maybe I do mind because the belt unbuckling is making me nervous. I think I'd be okay with a fun hand spanking, but I'm not sure how I feel about being smacked with a belt. "With your belt?"

He pauses, glancing between where his hands are unzipping his pants and my face. "I'd prefer not to, but I suppose I could if that's what you need to get off."

"No, thank you."

"No, thank you?" He smiles and shakes his head as his pants drop to the floor. "Jesus, I can't with you."

"Few can," I agree and roll over, pushing up onto my knees and forearms before glancing at him again over my shoulder. I'm down for a bit of doggy style. It's not what I asked for, but I really am more adaptable than I'm given credit for.

"You are the bossiest, most aggravating woman I've ever met."

"Tell me something I don't already know."

"I didn't fuck you last night because you were drunk."

"So were you," I shoot back.

His hands wrap around my waist and he pulls me towards him until my knees are on the edge of the bed, my feet dangling over the side. I grip the bedspread in my fingers and wiggle my ass a little in invitation. His palms smooth over my skin before he runs one of them up my spine. Slowly, from ass to nape. I shiver and hold back a moan, mostly because I fear it would sound like I'm faking it and I'm not. I'm so not. I could probably come from nothing more than Vince running his hands across my skin. His touch makes me shiver in all the best ways, my skin heating beneath his touch, goosebumps trailing in the path of his fingertips.

Then his fist winds in my hair and suddenly I'm pulled upright, one hand on my hip to keep me steady as he lowers his lips to my ear. His fist tightens in my hair as he tilts my head a fraction to the side, his breath warm against my skin when he speaks.

"Do you always behave so stupidly, Payton?" The words are said softly, but seriously.

"Can you be more specific?"

"Do you often find yourself drunk and alone with men you hardly know?" His hand slides forward from my hip, his fingers splaying out across my stomach, the middle two resting a fraction above where I want them most.

"No, never."

"Yet you did last night."

"Yes."

"Why?"

"I trusted you," I murmur. Now is probably not the time to mention my theories on fate, because this feels like some kind of kinky lie detector test and I'm liable to say more than I'd like to with his fingers inching south.

Then he bites my earlobe and dips his hand between my thighs. Two fingers spread me open as his middle finger glides across my wet center. Up and down, teasing my opening before retreating to circle my clit. Around and around. It makes my knees weak and I'd probably fall out of his embrace if not for the hand fisting my hair and the forearm pressed against my stomach.

"It was stupid, Payton. Reckless. And I won't have it."

Oh, hells yes. He's heard me on the dirty talk request and he's raised the bar with some alpha male bullshit. I love alpha male bullshit, but only if the guy can pull it off. If they can't pull it off you end up in the midst of a very awkward exchange in which you're asked if you've been a bad girl and you have to tell him to stop talking.

Vince can talk all day long as far as I'm concerned.

He kisses the spot behind my ear, his lips moving down my neck as his fingertip slides inside of me. He rims my entrance with slow, confident strokes, stretching and stroking with perfection.

"This pussy is mine now," he breathes into my ear. "For however long you're mine you'll behave accordingly. I won't have you taking unnecessary risks with yourself, Payton."

Belongs to him? Have I just entered a kinky time portal to nineteen-twenty?

I don't exactly hate it.

"Are we clear?"

"Yes." Clear enough. His finger is back to manipulating my clit like it's the only job that finger was born to do, so who really gives a fuck about clarity? Not me. I'm not the head of the clarity oversight committee. I'm not even on the task force.

"You're driving me crazy." He brushes his lips against my ear when he says it. He growls the word a little and I'm not sure if it's a good crazy or a bad crazy. 'Crazy' is a word that can be used to describe passion and arousal and infatuation. But it's also a word used to describe what it feels like to be stuck in a traffic jam or an actual lunatic. "I don't do crazy, Payton. Ever. I do order and logic and reason and you are none of those things."

"I might grow on you though."

I'm almost positive I can feel his lips smiling against my neck before he releases my hair and pushes me down until my elbows are on the bed once again. He slides his hands up and down my spine, pausing at the small of my back to massage his thumbs across my skin in a soothing firm circular motion. Then he continues over my hips, hands gliding down my thighs before he uses them to spread my bent knees farther apart.

Then he... holy shit, he licks me. From behind. Top to bottom before covering me with his mouth. Oh. My. God. I think my new husband might be the head of the oral Olympic committee. I've always considered myself pretty outgoing sexually, but honestly this never even occurred to me as an option. Thank fuck I'm facing the mattress because I know my mouth is hanging open like a gaping goldfish and I might possibly be cross-eyed.

Holy. Hell.

I drop my chest to the bed because I can't possibly hold myself up. He laughs and oh, sweet Jesus, his scruff-covered chin is rubbing directly against my clit and I might die. He's fucking me with his tongue while his chin bangs my clit and that's it, I'm dead. I'm nothing but heat and pressure and pulsations and it's all in one spot. Every nerve ending in my body right now has relocated between my thighs, I'm certain of it. I could slam my hand in a door and feel nothing except the pleasure between my legs because there's no room to feel anything else.

I should be thinking things right now, like how his nose is literally pressed against my asshole in this position, but fuck, he's so into it I don't care. Or about how I'm so wet his face must be covered with me, but again, I don't care. The sum total of things I care about is the orgasm building inside of me. The feel of his lips when he sucks on my clit. The rimming of his tongue around my entrance. The brush of his scratchy jaw in my most delicate of places. The swipe of his tongue between my pussy and asshole. The nip of his teeth on my—oh, my God. That's it, right there. Right there. I'm shaking and making weird noises and I think there might be tears coming out of my eyes. I'm glad I'm face down on the bed because I'm so light-headed I think I might black out. That felt like pleasure detonating inside of me. Like an orgasm bomb.

He pinches my ass as he stands and just like that I'm ignited and needy all over again. Sated, yet horny. Hmm, that would be such a good name for a band. Or a sex toy shop. Then he tells me to move to the center of the bed so I do, crawling forward a few lengths before turning onto my back to watch him.

He's sliding his underwear past his knees, and when he stands his cock stands with him. Erect and bobbing for attention. Penises are sorta ridiculous in general, but I find his magnificent. I saw it last night in the shower—hell, I had my hands wrapped around it in the shower—but seeing it again makes me clench in need. Did I mention it's big? It is. Big. I thought maybe I'd enlarged the memory of it through my tequila tinted glasses but no, it's impressive.

"I like your penis," I mention in case that scores me a point on the good side of the crazy ledger he might be keeping. One point in the fun crazy column for liking his penis. Ten points in the bad crazy column for this marriage débacle. Shit. That math is not adding up in my favor. I wonder how many points anal would be worth?

"I know."

Fuck my life, if I sang a penis song last night he is never going to take me seriously.

"Specifically how do you know?" I turn on my side and trace my fingertip over the bedspread.

"You've mentioned it a few times." He drops a hand to his length as he speaks, stroking himself with his fist. I freaking love it when men do that, as if they give no fucks that they're pumping themselves right in front of you. He twists his wrist at the tip before sliding back to the base and he's not gentle with his motions. "'I like your penis,'" he begins to sing in that voice he uses that's supposed to sound like me. My eyes widen in alarm and fly to his but he's already laughing and shaking his head. "Just kidding."

This guy.

He's smiling and stroking his monster cock and giving me that look he gives me like he finds me interesting and he's doing it all at the same time. Not for nothing, but I might have a special gift for picking near strangers to marry. Like a sixth sense.

Except that I think the sixth sense is an extrasensory perception so I'm not sure I'm using that idea correctly. Or maybe I am? Whatever, you get the gist.

Vince snags the condom off the bed and rips it open with his teeth before rolling it over the length of him. My heart is pounding when he crawls over me, resting between my spread legs as he kisses me, his cock heavy against my stomach. I ache for wanting him. Wanting him inside me, stretching me, claiming me, using me for his pleasure. I roll my hips beneath him as I tug on the ends of his hair, trying to pull him closer. But then he's easing back. Kneeling between my thighs, starting at my wet needy center.

Then he lifts one of my legs and bends it back, my bent knee resting in the crook of his elbow as he spreads me wider open.

"Where do you want it, Payton?" He slaps the tip of his cock against my mound as he asks. "You didn't say exactly where you wanted it. Should I put it here?" He nudges against my asshole with the tip of his cock and I clench out of reflex.

"You can," I offer.

"You think you could take me this way?" He raises a brow in challenge, the tip of him pressing just enough to feel a slight burn, but not enough to make any real progress.

"I don't actually. You're really big and I think we'd need more than a sample packet of lube to make that happen. But I assume you know better than I do."

His eyes flash, twin pools of heat and desire and warning.

"I'm a traditional fucker, Payton. I like to start with pussy." He moves the head of his cock up and I feel him parting me with the tip, pushing inside just enough for me to feel the pressure of him. The heat and weight and mass of him.

"Is that what you call what you just did with your mouth?" I challenge. "Traditional?" I wiggle my hips, trying to get more of him inside of me. I'm not sure why I'm encouraging him to hurry because a cock that size should be treated with a little respect. It's just that I'm not the most levelheaded of girls in the best of circumstances and we're going on twenty-four hours of foreplay. I'm ready to change my band name from Sated, Yet Horny to Flash Flooding.

He shakes his head and murmurs something about my mental health before flexing his hips on a quick thrust. I wouldn't call it a slam so much as a perfectly-aimed nine-ball in the corner pocket. If the nine-ball was a bit too wide for the pocket but the pocket had stretching abilities and enjoyed a challenge.

I exhale and ease the bedding from my grip.

"You good?" Vince is watching me closely.

"Hmm-hmm," I murmur and nod my head, watching him back. He really is the most attractive man I've ever laid eyes on. I reach up and trace my fingertip over his bottom lip. I cannot believe I get to do this with him. It's like winning the sex lottery, I think as I wiggle my hips beneath him.

"You feel so fucking good," he groans and pulls back before sinking back into me.

"Same," I reply, tightening around him.

"Hands above your head," he instructs as he moves my leg to his shoulder. Oh, holy Jesus, that changes things a little. I bend my other leg to brace my foot on the bed because I think I'm going to need it. And then he's moving faster, and it's rough and hot and deep, just like I asked for. I don't even think about moving my hands from because I need them where they're at to keep to keep a safe distance between my head and the headboard.

Vince pinches my nipple and I tighten so hard around the length of him we both hiss in response.

"Fuck, you're so tight," he whispers in my ear. "Tight and wet. You feel even better than I imagined you would."

You know what turned me on the most in that sentence? The idea of him thinking about fucking me. I moan deep in my throat and rotate my hips to meet his thrusts.

"Ditto," I whisper back.

"You're even wetter on my dick than you were on my face."

If I was capable of blushing, I would. I mean I am. Capable of it. But I'm already so flushed and breathless I don't think a blush would be discernible right now.

Then he bends both of my knees to my chest, my feet resting on his shoulders, and sinks back into me.

"Oh, my God."

"Yes," he coaxes "Talk to me. Tell me what you like."

"I like you," I say because it's really the only way to sum up my feelings. I've never been with anyone like him before. He's like some magical combination of accommodating and aggressive and it's totally my jam.

He's so deep and the pressure is so intense. It's building and building and I feel like I'm just a mass of particles and tension ready to explode. I can hear myself, his name falling from my lips in repetition, over and over. My neck arched, my fingers digging into his forearms.

It feels so good to be filled by him like this. He's so deep it's nearly painful, yet I don't want him to stop. He's hitting all the right places in this position and I'm so close that the nip of pain when he thrusts deep only serves to push me closer to where I want to go.

"You feel so good, Payton." He's breathing heavily and I know he's close. I know he's holding back for me. "I can't wait to feel you come on my cock. Fuck, you're so slick and hot, you feel so good."

When I come it feels like it lasts forever. I'm not even sure if it's still Sunday. It could be sometime next week or maybe I really have time-traveled back to nineteen-twenty. I have no idea.

"Jesus Christ." Vince slides my ankles from his shoulders until my legs are flat on the bed, spread open to accommodate him where he's still buried inside of me.

Boring missionary style, if you will. And I'm not even helping because I'm boneless and sated and in no control of my limbs.

Then he kisses me and it's not boring at all. His forearms are braced beside my head, holding some of his weight off of me. His hands are cupped under my head, and he kisses me like he means it. Like he's not just fucking some random wife he picked up last night. He pumps into me several more times until he finds his own orgasm and he's beautiful when he does. God help me, he's so beautiful I am ruined for ever watching another man come.

When he's done, after he's pulled out of me and gotten off the bed to dispose of the condom, he comes back. He comes back and he pulls me on top of him so that my head is resting on his chest, his fingers wrapping around a lock of my hair. "I like it wavy," he says, running his fingers through the tangled mess.

If he hadn't already ruined me with the two most perfect orgasms of my life, this moment would have done the trick all on its own. This simple moment of intimacy, the feel of his bare chest under my cheek, his heartbeat in my ear, the gentle caress of his fingers.

Sex is weird. Why did I think this was a good idea? Would it have killed me to think something all the way through for once? Before diving in headfirst and making it worse?

Is it better to have fucked and lost than never to have fucked at all?

Not fucked is the answer here.

Not fucked, because I'd have been better off not knowing how good we were together. It'd make what comes next so much easier to handle.

Right on cue, he ruins it. Exactly like I knew he would.

"We need to talk about last night."

FIFTEEN

SOMETIMES FATE DOES me a solid. Like right now, because my phone has chosen this exact moment to sound an alarm. Why I've got an alarm set for Sunday afternoon, I've no idea, but my phone is annoyingly chiming from the kitchen all the same.

See? Fate.

I slide out of Vince's embrace with a, "Hold on," then slip my t-shirt over my head as I dash into the other room to grab it because there is nothing more agitating than the alarm tone on a phone. Then I see what the alarm was for.

Life coaching. I've got a life coaching appointment in fifteen minutes. Fine, it's Meghan's life coaching session if you want to be bogged down by the tiny details, but I think we can all agree that I could really use some guidance. Honestly there's probably not a person in the greater Las Vegas metropolitan area who needs it more than me.

Why on earth did I set an alarm only giving me a fifteen-minute warning? Obviously I assumed I was going to be dressed at one forty-five in the afternoon or I'd have set the alarm to go off earlier. Crap, I don't have much time. And if I miss this appointment I won't know when the next appointment is because it's not like I can reschedule.

That settles it, I really have to go.

"I have a thing!" I announce as I run back into my bedroom. "An appointment. I'm sorry, I've got to run. I'm so late!" I slide my underpants up my legs in what must be the least sexy exit in the history of fleeing the consummation of a marriage ever to have occurred. This is followed by the classic hop-hop-hop to get my yoga pants pulled over my ass.

So sexy.

I'm sure I already ruined any fantasy Vince could possibly have had about marrying a sex vixen when I told him I drank Gatorade in the shower, so no point dwelling on it now anyway.

Vince pulls himself to sitting in the bed with a huff and a sigh and is now rubbing his temples with his fingers. Fucking drama llama. I snap my bra up from the floor but decide I don't have time to deal with it so I just loop it over my arm and then swipe all the things spread across my dresser back into my tiny clutch. Minus the condoms and lube because I've learned my tiny purse lesson and I won't be needing those.

I stuff my feet into the first pair of flip flops I come across then whirl back towards Vince, bra in one hand, clutch in the other. "We will talk"—I point the bra hand at him before realizing it's my bra hand—"later," I add once I've tucked the bra hand to my chest.

Vince leans back against my headboard, watching me. He's not attempted to interrupt my blathering, just watched quietly as I moved through the room like a whirlwind on my way out the door. I'm not sure what he's thinking because he's not saying anything and he's got a really great resting neutral face. A resting neutral face is when you are unable to guess what that person is thinking because they're not giving you any obvious facial cues and you are not a mind reader.

I know, I know. I could... ask. I could ask him what he's thinking. Talk to him. Behave like the adult my driver's license claims me to be. I just need a second to think and I've got this appointment and—I'm a jerk.

A jerk with twelve minutes to crash another life coaching session.

In case you're wondering, I do manage to put my bra on in the car. It's a pretty magical feat that requires a whole lot of fidgeting, some extraordinary stretching and a long red light, but it's on. I make it to Grind Me with two minutes to spare, throw my car into park and run inside. In my yoga pants, t-shirt, flip flops and my clutch from last night.

I'm such a hot mess.

Carol the life coach is already at a table with a cup of something in front of her. Meghan has a drink in hand and is just about to sit down.

Okay, play this cool. I stroll up to the counter like I'm not in a hurry and order an iced coffee. Then I change it to just a regular ole cup of hot coffee because that's faster and I don't want to miss the first few minutes of Meghan's meeting waiting on a barista. I do stop long enough to add cream and sweetener because I can't talk myself into drinking black coffee no matter how much of a hurry I'm in.

Then I slip into an empty table next to Carol and Meghan. That's when I realize I've forgotten my headphones. I've also forgotten to grab a stack of napkins, so I can't pretend to be an artist crafting the next great American novel on coffee shop napkins because I'm too precious or pretentious to type. I don't have a pen in this handbag anyway, so I've failed on all counts. Which leaves me with... being a weirdo in a coffee shop.

You know those people? The ones who sit in coffee shops and drink coffee? Alone. Without a laptop, a book, a newspaper, a notebook, or headphones? Everyone knows those people are weird, just sitting there drinking their coffee in a coffee shop. Hey, I appreciate the irony too, but I'm not in charge of what's considered weird. I'm not the weird police. Thankfully I have my phone with me so I can pretend I'm texting. It's still weird but I'll have to make do.

Or.

Or I could leave. Go home. Leave Meghan to have her life coaching session in the privacy of a half-filled coffee shop. Talk to Vince. Sort out how one goes about annulling a marriage. It can't be that hard, right? It wasn't that hard to get married last night, I can promise you that. There wasn't even a line at the marriage bureau office. Just us and we breezed in and out, easy-peasy. Might have been because they were closing in five minutes and wanted to get rid of us, but it was easy nonetheless.

Looking back, you'd have thought we'd have come to our senses during the cab ride to get the marriage license, but alas, we did not. My memory of that ride is nothing but a blur of back-seat groping I haven't seen the likes of since high school. I think it was me doing most of the groping because I have a memory of Vince whispering, "Patience, sweets," in my ear.

He's so damn cute.

If I can use cute as a word to describe the sexiest, most virile man I've ever been in the back seat of a car with.

Anyway.

I should probably skip this life coaching thing and go find Vince. He's probably still getting dressed or rifling through my stuff. I'm not even mad if he is because I'd be looking through his stuff if he'd left me alone in his place.

I wonder if there's an annulment bureau office? Maybe this will be easy? Maybe we just go down to the annulment bureau office and sign an annulment license and voilà, it's undone? Then he'll realize I'm not completely nuts and really sort of fun and charming in my own way. He'll ask me to dinner and we'll live happily ever after.

There's probably a line at the annulment bureau office though. A long annoying line that will give him too much time to think about the fact that he's only known me a day and I've already caused him nothing but chaos. Chaos and orgasms. And I'm the one who's had the majority of the orgasms, so I'm not sure that's a selling point unless he's got a thing for giving more than he receives. I should try to woo him a little before we dissolve this marriage though, or he might think an annulment is a hard breakup when really we're just getting started because we have so much potential together.

Right?

Otherwise what was the point of all of this? It's not random. It cannot be random that I'd see him and feel things and then bam, I walk into Double Diamonds with Lydia and there he is. All that energy and lust between us cannot be random biology. That's fate. Or the universe recognizing two souls meant to unite, blah, blah, blah.

Besides, we all know that 'random' is just a dull word for 'fortuitous.' If nothing else this has been a series of fortuitous events that will lay out the course for the rest of my life. And Vince's. And our future children's. Sorry to get ahead of myself, but it's impossible not to look at him and think about the possibilities of commingling our DNA.

The possibilities are adorable, by the way. I'm envisioning they'll all have dark hair and dark eyes just like Vince. Maybe one of them will look like me, a tiny blonde toddler with wavy hair and big blue eyes that she'll use against us to get whatever she wants.

Us. There's no us, I remind myself. There's not, but maybe there could be? Vince looks at me like he gets me. Like he sees me. Do you know how rare that is? For anyone to really look at you past a cursory glance? To look at you like they see the real you? Like they want to know more than what you're saying, they want to know what you're thinking about too?

It's rare. Like it's never happened to me before Vince. Not like this. Most people, when you tell them you sang a taco song as a child because you believed that's where tacos came from—from the song—would laugh. They wouldn't ask you to sing it. They definitely wouldn't remember all the words the next day and bring you tacos.

I slap my fingers against my forehead. I cannot believe I told him about the taco song. I told him a lot of things last night.

That's when I tune in to Carol asking Meghan where she sees herself in five years. I always thought that question was a dumb cliche. Like no one really walks around asking people something so obnoxious, right?

Yet Carol's asking. She's really bringing the hard-hitting questions to the Grind Me café on a Sunday afternoon.

You know where I'll be in five years? Divorced. Annulled, whatever. I'll be twenty-seven and divorced. Hell, I might be divorced two or three times by then, who knows.

You know where I'll be in twenty-five years? Mailing wedding invitations to my children. Just like my parents.

I should call my mom and ask her if her first marriage was to a complete stranger she had strong lustful feelings for. A man who made her want to do crazy things like believe in love at first sight and happily ever afters. A man who made her heart race and her stomach fill with swans. I know butterflies is the word everyone uses for that feeling, but swans mate for life so wouldn't a stomach full of swans make more sense? Besides, did you know that female butterflies mate only once and then die as soon as they lay their eggs, while male butterflies flitter around mating with as many females as they can find until they run out of sperm?

The more you know, right?

Vince gives me a stomach full of swans.

I wonder if my mom's first husband made her feel like doing crazy things in the hopes that he'd get it, that he'd catch her. That he'd want to be a little crazy right alongside of her.

I wonder if my mom's first marriage felt like serendipity but ended in heartache. I've never asked much about that guy. I was ten before I even comprehended that my father wasn't her first marriage, he was her second. They'd long since divorced by then and she was newly engaged. A relative had made an offhand comment about the third time being a charm and my life had tilted off its axis a bit. Third? She'd had a life before the union that produced me? A husband before my father?

Looking back I have no idea why it was unfathomable to me. I have an older brother courtesy of my father's first marriage. I'd always understood that my dad had been married before, but the idea that my mom had also been married before had thrown me for a loop. The feeling had been much like discovering that Santa wasn't real. I'd figured that one out during the Christmas of my seventh year when "Santa" had duplicated two of his gifts at both my mom's and dad's houses. The old man made a list and checked it twice, but he couldn't figure out how to split my presents in half and drop them in two different locations without error? And why did Santa have to make two stops just because my parents couldn't live in the same house? It didn't add up to me.

I'd called bullshit.

'Bullshit' is a word that adults don't like to hear from a seven-year-old's mouth. My dad confiscated my new Lego set as punishment. It'd taken everything in me not to roll my eyes and point out that I'd *just* explained that I had the exact same thing back at Mom's house, so as far as punishments go, it was dumb.

Meghan doesn't tell Carol any of this, obviously, since this is her appointment and not mine. Meghan tells her about her career aspirations and a timeshare she wants to buy in Mexico.

"What about your personal goals?" Carol asks and Meghan falters.

I feel you, Meghan. I feel you hard.

"You have issues with intimacy," Carol tells

Meghan and my heart stops because so do I! Who runs out of a post-cuddle session with a sex god? No one. No one does that. Not even if the sex god is their brand-new husband whom they've known for something under thirty hours. A well-adjusted normal person would never run. Granted, a well-adjusted normal person wouldn't be in that situation to begin with, but still. He was playing with my hair and telling me he likes it just the way it is—without a time-consuming blow dry—and I ran out.

Speaking of blowing, I am blowing this all the blows. He probably won't even want to date me after our annulment, which is going to be a real big problem for me because my ovaries strongly believe he's meant to father my children and you can't fight biological urges, it's like trying to fight with fate. Perhaps I'd be able to fight the lust if he was annoying, but he's not. He's so not. Everything about him draws me in, makes me want more.

I know, I know. I've known him like ten minutes.

Crazy person, table of one.

"Your life isn't randomly happening to you," Carol is telling Meghan. "Your life is a compilation of the choices you make, both emotional and logical. Leave space for both. Don't let your head talk your heart out of something you really want."

Gah, Carol is so wise. I'm really glad I found her.

"Leave room for the unexpected, Meghan."

Right, right, right.

Then Carol starts droning on about changes in the real-estate market and leaving room for growth in income properties. Then I miss a bunch of it because a group of teenagers have descended onto a nearby table so I'm now getting a mix of life coaching and homecoming plans.

In any case, I'm starting to wonder if Meghan and I want the same things out of these sessions. Still good advice though.

Carol and Meghan wrap up their meeting, agreeing to meet again on Thursday. I stay for an extra half hour because I am procrastinating like a boss and also because these homecoming plans are quite dicey.

When I get back to my apartment Vince is gone and I'm melancholy. The taco mess is gone too, the table cleared. The plastic cup from my iced coffee has been rinsed and placed in the recycle bin. He's basically killing it as a husband. Good in bed, cleans up after himself, recycles.

In my bedroom the stuffed shark has been placed back onto my pillow. I take him with me to the sofa where I spend the remainder of the day binge-watching a reality show in which strangers paired up by relationship experts agree to marry each other at their first meeting. I'm not sure which is crazier, marrying a stranger you picked out yourself, or marrying a stranger a team of relationship experts picked out for you. I decide it's a toss-up but it does make me feel better about my life choices.

SIXTEEN

"WHAT'D YOU DO THIS weekend?" It's Monday and I'm at my desk working on quoting a wedding for next fall. I'd like to tell the client that they can get this entire package on a much smaller and more neon-lit scale at a variety of chapels across Las Vegas, but I like having a job so instead I input the numbers for a balloon drop as requested.

"I married the hot guy from the lobby."

"Sure, sure." He nods. "Do you have time to create a room block for the Swanson event before lunch?"

I stop typing and pull the decoy rings from my finger, the ones I have stacked next to my wedding band so that it's not obvious I'm wearing a wedding band. Then I lift my hand up to Mark's face and wiggle my fingers.

"You did not!" Mark's eyes widen, then narrow as if he can't quite determine if I'm serious or playing an elaborate joke on him.

"I did. Don't tell Lydia, she doesn't know."

"Huh," Mark replies. His mouth opens then closes without any words coming forth.

I nod.

"So"—he draws the word out slowly—"married?"

"Married."

"Isn't that something."

123

"It's something all right."

"So what are you gonna do?"

"What do you mean?" I bristle, turning away to stick my decoy rings back on. "Fifty percent of marriages end in divorce, it's not like people who get married on purpose know what they're doing either."

"That is one way of looking at it."

"Right?" I tap my pen against my desk, excited about this loophole. "Statistically I'm in good shape, don't you think?"

"Sure, sure." Mark nods along in the way one does when they're humoring a crazy person.

"I've totally got my shit together, Mark. In fact, I created a room block for the Swanson event an hour ago and emailed it to you. So there." I think marriage really suits me. For example, this morning I had a banana for breakfast instead of Cheez-Its and just now I sent that thing to Mark because I knew he needed it before he even asked. I think I've matured this weekend. It feels quite satisfying.

"Thank you for the email. I enjoyed the link to the new eyeshadow palette from Urban Decay."

"Oh, crap. I included the wrong link?" Why am I such a disaster?

"Yup."

I turn back to my keyboard and open a new email to Mark, attaching the correct link this time. Copy-pasting links can be the devil itself but at least I didn't send him a link to porn. That would never happen, but only because I don't use my work computer to look at porn.

"What in the hell are these?" Mark is holding one of the badges I made for Lydia last night, a look of confusion on his face. I can't blame him because the badges are fairly ridiculous, if I'm using 'ridiculous' as a word that means 'made of awesome.'

"Life achievement badges for Lydia," I reply with a glance at the clock. I'm meeting her for lunch in ten minutes so I need to get moving. The employee cafeteria is a six-minute walk from my desk, because this place is huge. "It helps motivate her to complete adult tasks if she earns a badge," I explain even though it's obvious.

"Uh-huh." Mark squints.

"Gimme." I hold out my hand palm up. "I've got to meet her for lunch. I'm going to try the salad bar today because I'm married now and that's the kind of bar married people hang out in."

"That sounds right." He slaps the badges into my palm. "Have fun."

Fuck my life, salad bars are depressing. I stare at the pile of lettuce, cucumbers and green pepper on my plate and wonder if this step of adulthood is really necessary. The only thing that can salvage this is cheese. And ranch dressing. I slide my tray down the line and examine the rest of my options. I wonder if I like chickpeas? I wonder if Vince likes chickpeas? I wonder what the hell he does all day at the strip club?

Seriously though.

Is he reviewing invoices for toilet paper and replacing burnt-out neon light bulbs?

Doubtful.

I should probably learn how to pole-dance, take an interest in his interests. That would be a super wifely thing to do, wouldn't it? I drop four servings' worth of croutons onto my salad, then go off in search of Lydia. She's already got a table so I plop down across from her with a huge grin. I cannot wait to hear about her weekend.

"So"—I dive straight in—"how was it?"

By "it," I mean sex.

Lydia blushes, fidgets and bites her lip.

"Good," she says, looking anywhere but at me.

"Good? That's it?" Lydia's inability to gossip is even more disappointing than this salad I'm eating. I've been looking forward to hearing the dirty details all weekend. Being nosey is such a burden at times, but I sigh and press on. "We're both talking about sex, right? The sex was good?"

"So good." Lydia's fighting back a smile, her lips twisting.

"On a scale of one to hung, what are we talking about size-wise?" I hold up my hands, palms facing each other, and draw them apart, then closer, then apart again, waiting for her to tell me when to stop. "Was it smaller or larger than average?" I suspect Rhys is packing. I don't want to brag but I'm a pretty good dickstimater. A dickstimater is a word for someone who is good at guessing dick size.

"I can't tell you that!"

"Right. Because you've only seen the one dick and you don't have anything to compare it to. Just tell me if it was longer or shorter than a stick of butter."

"Longer."

"Thicker or thinner than a can of Coke?"

"Thinner! It felt like a can of Coke, but definitely thinner. Oh, my God, I can't believe I just said that." Lydia gasps and slaps a hand over her eyes. I laugh and pull out the badges I've made for her. I've got a blow job badge, a sex badge and a butt stuff badge. I place them on the table in a row between us lined up in a row.

"You made badges!" She beams, peering over my handiwork before sliding the sex badge off the table and running it between her fingers. "This is very nice work, Payton." The girl really does love her badges. She fingers the other two with the tip of her finger before pushing them back in my direction. "I haven't earned these yet," she says and I know it kills her a little bit because she's an overachiever.

"He didn't want a blow job?" I'm appalled.

Except. Except Vince didn't let me give him a blow job this weekend either. Good Lord, maybe blow jobs have gone out of style? Hahah. Honestly, I crack myself up.

"He said not till Wednesday," Lydia replies like that's a thing.

"Excuse me?" I spear a cucumber with my fork and drag it through the ranch dressing before popping it into my mouth.

"I don't know." Lydia shrugs. "That's what he said."

"Hmm," I hum around the cucumber in my mouth. God, I really am funny. Also, I need to hum on Vince's dick, pronto.

"So what did you do this weekend?" Lydia asks. "Besides make badges for me?"

"Oh, you know. The usual." *Married Vince,* I want to say. I want to tell her everything and get her advice, but now isn't really the time. Everything is so new for her with Rhys and I don't want to make it all about me. Maybe I can just talk around it a little? I stab a green pepper with my fork while I contemplate how I can talk about this without really talking about this.

"Did you know, statistically speaking, arranged marriages have a much higher success rate than those of individuals who choose for themselves?" I chew on the green pepper as nonchalantly as possible. Green peppers taste like slivers of green ice and depression.

"I have heard that, yes," Lydia replies with a small laugh. "Were you binge-watching *Married at First Sight* again?"

More like living it.

"Maybe," I admit. "It could work though, don't you think?"

"Well, I suppose there is some merit to it."

"Right!"

"A team of psychologists could match suitable partners, I guess. They'd likely have a good handle on compatible personality traits, and they're matching people who are actively seeking a life partner, so everyone's goals are the same."

"Just like fate!" I nod my head as I say it.

"No, I don't think psychology and fate are anything alike." Lydia is shaking her head in response to my vigorous head-nodding.

"Hmm." Dammit.

SEVENTEEN

I'VE JUST GOTTEN HOME from work and changed into a tank top and pair of pajama pants Lydia made from an old sheet when there's a knock on my door. I think we all know who that is.

"Thank God you're here," I announce as I swing open the door. "I'm glad you finally came over. It's weird the way you've been avoiding me." I give him a cheeky grin as I eye him from head to toe. Sweet baby Jesus, does he look good. He's wearing a suit and tie and he still looks pressed even at the end of the day. Seeing him makes me flush all over with excitement and anticipation. Seeing him makes the swans in my stomach swim in rapid little circles. I don't know why, but he just does it for me. Destiny has done me a real solid in tossing him in my path, that's for sure.

He does that little headshake thing I'm already familiar with. Then he rolls his eyes at me for good measure.

"Cute," he mutters as he strolls past me. "Real cute."

He's carrying a brown paper grocery bag. The kind you get at the expensive grocery store because hipsters love retro and the environment. Vince is not a hipster so I can only assume he shops there because the groceries are fancy as fuck.

"You keep going on and on about how much you like me, but then you disappear. It's weird, right? You should really get your shit together before you give me a complex." I shake my head as I close the door behind him.

"Uh-huh," Vince mutters heading straight for my kitchen.

"Did you bring me groceries? Thank God, I'm starving. I had a salad for lunch, which sucked, by the way, and I ate the last of my Cheez-Its in the shower yesterday."

Vince pauses, the bag hovering over my countertop. "What?" He squints at me like I'm talking nonsense. Then he does a slow perusal of what I'm wearing and scowls. "So you're in your pajamas and you have no food in the house? What were you going to eat for dinner, Payton?"

"Um..." I wrinkle my nose, head tilted to the side. "I don't think it should come as any great surprise to you that I don't always think things though."

"Right." And with that he tosses the manila envelope he'd had tucked under his arm onto the countertop and begins unpacking the grocery bag. "You need to sign those, but first I'm making dinner and then we'll talk."

Fuckity fuck, that was fast. Apparently my husband doesn't lack initiative. Initiative is a trait that comes in handy when you need the trash taken out or a piece of furniture assembled. It's not a trait that comes in handy when you're trying to buy some time on your annulment. "Dinner, wow."

"I'm a very busy man, Payton. I'm multitasking."

"Of course. And we should talk. Absolutely," I agree as nonchalantly as possible while side-eyeing the hell out of the envelope. "So many things to talk about."

"You don't have anywhere to go this evening, I presume?" Vince asks, eyeing my pajamas again. I'm wearing my favorite of the sheet pajamas. Lydia made them out of a vintage sheet with a bright floral pattern. They're super obnoxious. I've paired them with a grey tank top that says 'I just want a hug,' underneath a sketch of a porcupine.

"Nope." I shake my head and wiggle the envelope with my fingertip. It's large, the size of a sheet of printer paper.

"Are you sure? Do you want to double-check your calendar? I'd hate for you to have to run off without a bra again."

"Don't be old. I put it on in the car."

"Glad to hear it. I'd hate to think of you running around Las Vegas without one." His gaze drops to my chest. I'm definitely not wearing a bra right now and my breasts are most definitely appreciating his appearance in my house. "I assumed you'd have a corkscrew?" Vince questions as he pulls a bottle of red from the bag. "Pots and pans?" He looks as though he's second-guessing the idea that I might own cookware. He'd be correct to second-guess it, but I live with Lydia so we should be good.

"What are you making?" I move behind the kitchen island to dig out the corkscrew for him, placing it on the countertop next to the bottle before scooting around him to grab the glasses.

"Chicken and pasta." He shrugs out of his jacket and hangs it on the back of a kitchen chair before tugging at the knot of his tie. "You okay there?" He smirks, likely because I've stopped what I was doing to watch this tie-undoing. There's something very,

very enticing about the flex of his fingers, the veins running along the back of his hands as he works to loosen the knot and pull the material free of his collar. Why is that so stupid hot? I need to get a grip or this night is going to end the same way the previous two nights ended.

Wait, that's what I want though, right? A night that ends in orgasms?

I do want that, but I want to talk too. Definitely. Maybe not about our pending separation, but things. I'd like to know how he feels about cats for example. And if he's read any good books lately. If he prefers the Summer Olympics or the Winter. What his favorite movie is. If Saturday night was the best or worst night of his life.

I know he likes tacos. And pizza. And cooking. And giving oral. I know he's not into tattoos because he married me to prevent me from getting one and I couldn't find any on him. I know he thinks before he speaks and I know he likes me, at least a little.

He thinks I'm funny. And exasperating. And bossy. And beautiful, he said that I was beautiful.

It's not the worst start in the history of starts, but I'd like to know more.

I pull out a stool and sit down at the island countertop so I can watch Vince work. It occurs to me once again what a shit wife I am. I don't cook. I don't give blow jobs. I haven't asked if he needs anything dropped off at the dry cleaner. I don't wear sexy lingerie. Maybe I should change? To be fair, the blow job thing is not my fault. I did offer that first night. I meant to yesterday but he distracted me with his tongue and that was that. Gah, I'm just the worst.

"What are you thinking about?"

"Giving you a blow job."

"Yeah?" Vince responds easily, as if we're talking about where the cutting board is. "Do you have a list of specific requirements for how you'd want that to happen?"

So he's open to the idea, is what I'm hearing. Maybe he'll want to date after the annulment and he'll fall in love with me? It'll make a great story for our grandchildren.

"You say that like I'm demanding."

"You are."

"I'm extremely easy-going! Everyone says so!" No one says that, actually. But it's probably just because it's never come up. It's not as if I go around asking people if they think I'm easy-going, but if I did, they'd say yes. Probably. At least everyone except Vince would.

"You have a very easy-going way of getting your own way," Vince states as he sets a pot of water on the stove to boil.

I suppose I can see where he might think that. That might even be a fair assessment. I'm really self-aware. I need to add that to my list of positive attributes.

"So for the blow job, can I tie you up?"

"No." The answer is firm, his lips twitching like the question was amusing.

Humph. "Can you tie me up?"

"How are you going to give me a blow job if you're tied up?"

Dammit! Worst. Wife. Ever. "I suppose without my hands it'd be more like you using my mouth to masturbate while I did nothing, wouldn't it?"

"What a visual you paint, Payton."

"You're still welcome to tie me up though. It

doesn't have to be tradesies."

"Tradesies," he mutters with a shake of his head, but he's smiling as he uncorks the wine and pours two glasses.

"So, where do you see yourself in five years, Vince?" Might as well dive in with the talking.

He looks up from rolling back his shirt sleeves, a look of confusion flashing across his face replaced with an amused narrowing of his eyes.

"Excuse me? Is this an interview?" He laughs, placing a pan on my stovetop before rummaging through my cabinets for a bottle of olive oil.

"This is serious. You'll be old and divorced. Think about that."

"An annulment doesn't count as a divorce. It doesn't count as anything."

"Try telling that to Britney. She's gonna have that nineteen-hour marriage on her Wikipedia page until she dies. Wikipedia, Vince. That's forever."

"Okay, whoa. Let's step back a moment here."

"Do you need a wife with benefits?" I press on, because taking a step back doesn't sound like it will get me anywhere.

"What exactly does that mean?"

"I have health insurance. Do you need health insurance? I could add you to my plan. It's very reasonable, adding a spouse only costs like an extra two hundred dollars a month. It's a really good plan, too. At least that's what Lydia told me and she works in Human Resources so she would know. I'm no benefits package expert."

"That's not what the term 'with benefits' means."

"Listen, in this case I think it's exactly what that means. Society is the one who turned the word 'benefit' into something dirty."

"So there'd be no sex in this exchange?"

"Don't be ridiculous. Of course there'd be sex."

"Did you just talk yourself into a circle?"

"Maybe." Dammit.

"Hmmm," Vince murmurs. He's slicing a tomato. He's got chicken simmering in a pan and the noodles are cooking. I take a sip of wine and watch him work. He's got a dishtowel slung over his shoulder, sleeves rolled back to his elbows, and I'd skip dinner and go straight to eating him for dessert if I wasn't so hungry. Stupid salad.

"What'd you have for lunch today?" I ask, because I really want to know. A cheeseburger? A protein shake? Homemade tuna salad on rye?

"I had a lunch meeting at the Palm and I had the salmon."

"With like..." I pause, not sure how to pry subtly. "Someone from your staff?" I might as well have asked what she was wearing.

"With a client."

Oh, a client. A high roller. Or tipper? What do they call a big spender in a gentlemen's club? Well, whatever they're called. It's interesting. I never imagined Vince wining and dining clients during the day.

"What about tax breaks?" I burst out. "Married couples get tax relief, right?"

"So you're suggesting a marriage of convenience? With sex?"

"Maybe?"

"I can't imagine anything about you would be convenient for me."

I mean, he's not wrong. I huff and run my fingertip around the rim of my wineglass.

"Eloping is kind of a sample though, right?"

"How's that?"

"Like a free trial? Like when Netflix wants you to try them out so they give you thirty days for free?"

"No." Vince shakes his head. "Eloping is nothing like that."

"How about like a sample at the grocery store? Like when they let you taste the cheese before you buy an entire big chunk of it?" I make a motion in the air with my free hand, attempting to indicate picking up a small bit of cheese with a toothpick, but I think it ends up looking more like I'm making a sock puppet.

"What?" Vince tosses something into the pan with the chicken before turning back to face me. "How is a cheese sample like marriage?"

"You know that saying? Why buy the cow when the milk is free? I did offer you the milk for free, if you'll recall. So really this is all on you."

Vince stares at me for a long moment then shakes his head. It's not a little shake though, it's a full headshake.

"I cannot fathom one single way answering that ends well for me," he mumbles to himself as he turns off the stove and drains the pasta.

I shrug and get a couple of plates out and set them on the countertop before grabbing two forks and a couple of paper towels that I fold diagonally in half like fancy napkins. Then I move our wineglasses to the table and sit, watching him finish up in the kitchen.

"Maybe eloping is like a test drive, except you're test-riding your spouse to see if they're a good fit?"

Vince's lips tug into a smirk. "I think that's what dating is for."

"Sure. Except the majority of marriages end in

divorce and the general assumption is that all those couples dated first."

"Right." He eyes me between dishing up two plates full of steaming pasta covered in some kind of cheesy chicken concoction with a tomato slice on top. Super fancy pants compared to anything I'd have served.

"Arranged marriages have a much higher rate of success and those couples didn't date at all! So I think my math-ing would tell us that dating is nearly irrelevant to the statistical odds of a successful marriage."

"So you're suggesting a social experiment in which strangers marry each other to see if the divorce rates improve any based on random pairings?"

"It wouldn't be totally random. It'd be based on mutual coveting." I grin but he doesn't say anything. "Coveting is a fancy word for 'lust,'" I add helpfully. "Passion? Ardor? Desire?"

"Deranged," he replies. "It's a fancy word for 'crazy.'"

EIGHTEEN

SINCE HE'S ALREADY divorcing me I set about clearing my entire plate when he serves up his chicken pasta dish. There's no reason to pretend I'm a delicate flower at this point, we're way past that. I'm also still harboring a little resentment over choosing that salad for lunch and too hungry to care.

"So good," I moan around a mouthful of pasta. "Did they let you sample this cheese you used or did you already know it was good?" I ask when I'm done chewing.

"I can't tell if you're serious or insane."

"I'm just a real good time."

"You're something," he agrees. He takes a sip of wine, observing me over the rim of the glass.

"Have you ever met anyone like me though?"

He pauses for a long time, watching me as if he's giving this some real thought. "No," he finally says. "No, I most definitely have not."

"Have you ever been married before, Vince?"

"No." He shakes his head, a single back-and-forth motion. I wonder if he thought about marrying Gwen. That was the name of the ex Staci mentioned.

"Yeah, me neither." I shrug. "I'm afraid I might be terrible at it."

"What makes you think that?"

"My parents are terrible at it."

"It's not genetic."

"No, but it's learned behavior, isn't it? That might be worse."

"You seem very much like a woman who can do anything she sets her mind to."

"Hmm." I like that. I like that a lot. "What about your parents? Are they still married?"

"They were never married."

"Oh." I stab my fork into a bite of chicken while I imagine all the possibilities of what that means. Maybe it's something very tragic, like his parents were madly in love but his father died while his mother was pregnant. Maybe he was on a military mission or in a car accident while on his way to pick up a crib. I wonder if it makes Vince sad, whatever it was. I take a bite and observe him, wanting to know more but sure I don't have any right to ask.

"My mother was a stripper and my father was no one worth mentioning," he says after a couple of minutes of silence as we ate. It's like he can see the curiosity swirling around in my brain. Or maybe he's already familiar with my vivid imagination and decided to nip whatever visions I was having in the bud.

"Oh." It takes me a moment to process what he said. "Was?" I question. "Is she, um... has she passed?"

"Yes." He doesn't look sad, exactly. Vince doesn't give away much, I've found, but there's a definite poignancy that flashes across his eyes, a quick blink. "It's been a long time."

"I'm sorry."

"Thank you."

"Did she teach you how to make this?" I stuff

another bite into my mouth. I wonder if he'd like to be roommates if nothing else. I am good at doing the dishes when Lydia cooks, so I'm not a total deadbeat roommate.

"Not this specifically"—he smiles—"but she taught me to be self-reliant. She used to tell me she was my mother, not my maid."

"Smart."

"She was. She would have liked you," he adds. Then he blinks, looking surprised that he said it, that he revealed something he hadn't meant to.

"Do you have any siblings?"

"No, it was just me and me and my mom."

"Where do you go at the holidays then? Thanksgiving? Christmas?"

"What?"

"If you don't have a mom? Or a family? Where do you go?"

He looks at me for a long moment like my questions fascinate him. I think they're pretty ordinary questions but maybe he's not used to being asked such things.

"I work a lot during the holidays. Sometimes if I'm"—he pauses here as if he's not sure how to phrase this part—"with someone, we might travel."

Right. When he's with someone. Someone who is not me.

"You can come here for Thanksgiving if you want. If you're not with someone, that is." I use my fingers to air-quote the word 'someone.' "If you're home, you can come over. I won't even ask you to cook, because Lydia will do everything. I'll probably peel the potatoes or something." I frown, thinking about how Thanksgiving is a couple months away and perhaps Lydia won't be making Thanksgiving dinner in our apartment. We'd planned on it, discussed it when we made the move to Nevada, deciding it would be too expensive to fly home and we wouldn't have enough vacation time to make it worth a trip. But things change and she might be officially living with Rhys by then. She might want to have Thanksgiving there, not here.

"Does peeling potatoes make you sad?"

"Ha, no." He's very observant of me, I've noticed. Observant in general. I like the way he pays attention to me. "I was just thinking that Thanksgiving might be at Rhys' place instead of here. I don't think he's going to want to part with her after spending an entire month with her, because she's amazing and Rhys isn't a total idiot. So who knows, she might be living with him permanently by then and they'll want to have Thanksgiving at their place instead of here. Which is fine." I wave a hand to indicate the fineness of the entire situation and add a little shrug with my shoulder because by fine, I mean it's only sort of okay, because I thought Lydia and I were living together this year. "Does Rhys have a real kitchen in his hotel suite, do you know?"

"He does. They all do. But I think they order everything from the hotel kitchen. They might just cater Thanksgiving."

"Oh, no. Lydia would stroke out before she allowed that to happen." I shake my head vigorously. "Girl Troopers don't cater. She'll be making pies from scratch and creating a centerpiece out of something she rescued from the Goodwill. But anyway, you can still come. I bet it'll be the best misfit Thanksgiving ever!"

"Thank you, I appreciate the invitation."

"You're welcome."

"Tell me how you got kicked out of the Girl Troopers."

"How do you know about that?" I drop my fork onto my empty plate and gape at him. I might joke about it, but only with certain people because I'm actually very sensitive about it. It's the Achilles' heel of my childhood.

"Canon told me."

"Canon knows! How does Canon know? Does everyone know?"

Vince's eyes spark, his lips pulled into a smirk. "I'm joking. You told me. The other night."

"Oh."

"So?" he prods. "Tell me."

"It's embarrassing." I slump in my seat.

Vince leans forward, bracing his elbows on the table and leveling me with a stare. "When I was eight, my mom took me to Disneyland. It was a really big deal because we didn't have a lot of money. By which I mean she couldn't afford a hotel in Los Angeles and tickets to the park, so we drove there and back in one day. Four hours each way in the car so she could give me an afternoon at Disney." He takes a sip of wine and shakes his head. "And then I punched Tigger in the nuts."

"What?" I laugh. "Why?"

"I was going in for a hug, but he moved and my arm was already in motion so bam! Right in the junk. I was fucking mortified, so I cried."

"Did you get kicked out for assaulting Tigger?"

"No, but I felt like I ruined our day. I was too embarrassed to explain to my mom why I did it so she thought I was acting like an over-tired little punk. Looking back, it's all so stupid. Why didn't I just explain what happened? To my eight-year-old self it was too mortifying to talk about so I just clammed up. It still makes me cringe."

He takes another sip of wine, raising his eyebrows over the rim of the glass as if to say, *Your turn.*

"Okay." I sigh. "Fine." I fidget in my seat a bit to get comfortable before I begin. "The first overnight camp was coming up. It was only one night but it was a huge deal, you know?" He nods. "We were going to earn a camping badge and stay in tents and it was just this huge deal." I wave my hands around to indicate the importance and scope of the event. "But it was fifty dollars. Fifty freaking dollars, I still remember that."

"Your parents couldn't afford it?"

"No." I shake my head. "They could. But they were divorced and turned it into a fight about money. My mom insisted my dad should pay for the overnight camp because it fell on his weekend. My dad insisted he paid child support to cover expenses like overnight camp and my mom should pay for it."

"How old were you?" Vince asks, a line furrowing his forehead.

"Seven."

"That's harsh, putting you in the middle."

"Yeah. I just wanted to sleep in a tent and eat a hot dog that I cooked myself. God, that stupid hot dog. I had a stick picked out." I glance at Vince because this part is especially humiliating to me for some reason, and I've never told it to anyone. "I found this stick in my backyard and in my seven-year-old mind it was the perfect stick to roast a hot dog at camp. I thought I was going to bring my own stick to camp, along with my sleeping bag, which is dumb, isn't it? I painted the end I was going to use as a handle with pink sparkly nail polish and kept it under my bed for a month."

"But you never got to use it."

"Nope." I shake my head. "My entire troop came back with camping badges and stories I wasn't included in. So I got this idea that if I could just get the camping badge it'd be almost the same as if I was there."

"Okay." Vince nods as if that logic made any sense.

"I had this keychain, it was a tiny stuffed gorilla, and Mandy Marshall was dying to have it. So I traded her, my keychain for her camping badge."

"Industrious." Vince smiles. I like the little lines that appear by his eyes when he smiles.

"It was all going well, until the next troop meeting when Mandy missed having her badge."

"Ahh."

"She cried and somehow it all ended with me getting kicked out for conduct unbecoming of a Girl Trooper. They said I wasn't Girl Trooper material. I was seven! The worst part was she kept my keychain. She attached it to her backpack and wore it to school for the rest of the year."

"Ouch."

"Right? I should have known better. She'd been a serious bitch since kindergarten but I was blinded by that stupid badge." I stand, stacking our plates on top of each other and bringing them over to the dishwasher.

"Did you just refer to a five-year-old as a bitch?" Vince is laughing now.

"Well she was seven at this point in the story, but yeah, I guess I did just tell you she was already a bitch at five. In any case, that's my humiliating story of being kicked out of the Girl Troopers. They referred to it as a badge pyramid scheme, by the way, which has irritated me to this day because it was a badge-for-sale scheme, there was no pyramid." I finish loading the plates into the dishwasher, then add the cutting board and knife Vince used while he was cooking and set the pan in the sink filled with an inch of hot soapy water to soak. I wipe down the counter, stalling as long as possible before reaching for the envelope.

I slide it off the countertop and it's not as heavy as I expected. I know we've only been married forty-eight hours but I somehow thought that would warrant a weightier amount of paperwork.

"Hey." Vince speaks up and I lift my eyes to his. "Let's play a game."

NINETEEN

"WANT TO?" HE'S moved from the table to my living area where he's examining a set of board games stacked on a shelf under my television. It's a motley assortment of boxes that Lydia has collected from trips to the Goodwill. We haven't actually played any of them, but it pleases her to collect them. They're usually missing pieces, the boxes torn and taped. Sometimes she'll buy the same game a few times to get enough pieces to reassemble one complete game.

"What?" He wants to stay... and play a board game?

"How about Scrabble?"

"You're not too busy? You have time?" I set the envelope back onto the counter and eye him from where I'm standing in the kitchen.

He digs the box out from the stack and holds it up, the wooden pieces clattering about the box with the movement.

"I'm not sure if all the correct letters are in there. There may be twenty M's and no P's for all I know, my roommate bought that used."

"I'm willing to risk it." He opens the box and sets the board on the coffee table, then begins flipping all the pieces face down inside the lid. I abandon the envelope and walk slowly over to the sofa to join him, not quite believing that this is happening right now.

I draw the highest letter and start us off with the word SHARK. He smiles and uses the A in my word to play the word CRAZY.

It's nice, sitting here with Vince. He asks me what it was like growing up in Tennessee and what brought me to Las Vegas. I ask him what it was like to grow up in a desert. We don't keep score, just play and talk, and it's... nice. It's great.

I use the M from MIST to spell KISMET. It's not a particularly high-scoring word, which doesn't matter because we're not counting, but I'm very pleased with myself all the same.

"Kismet," he says softly as I lay down the tiles.

"It's a fancy word for fate!" I explain, thinking he's challenging the word like he did when I tried to play MATHING.

He kisses me.

I'm not expecting it. He's quietly looking at me one moment, his lips are pressed against mine the next. When his lips leave mine I sense he's just as surprised by the impromptu kiss as I am. The pad of his thumb trails my bottom lip, a soft firm exploration. Then he kisses me again, firmer now. Tongues mingling, hands exploring. I tug his head closer, my hands dragging through his hair. He pulls me closer, his hand cupping the nape of my neck.

Then I'm sitting astride him, one knee on each side of his hips. I kiss him everywhere. Brows and jaw. I run my tongue along the side of his neck and nip his earlobe with my teeth. His hands are roaming my back, cupping my bottom and slipping beneath my tank top.

It's the most satisfying make-out session I've been involved in since high school, except it's better because in high school I wasn't making out with grown men who knew what they were doing and I didn't have my own apartment. One of his hands works its way to my chest, and it's stupid really, that this one point of contact, his thumb brushing across my nipple as his lips press against my neck, should make me feel so many things. Turned on and safe and eager and wanted and excited.

I trail my fingertips down the sides of his neck before moving them to the second button on his shirt. The first one was undone when he took off his tie, but I need more of him exposed. I slip two additional buttons free of the fabric, freeing enough space to trace his clavicle, the sinewy spots where his neck muscles connect to his shoulders.

His hand leaves my breast long enough to slide my tank up. It's odd how something so simple can feel so erotic when Vince is doing it. It feels like my tank is coming off in slow motion, the material sliding up my stomach, his hands guiding the fabric on its journey. My skin tingles in the wake of his fingers as the material clears my chest, my arms lifting to allow the tank to clear my head. My hair falls in a wave against my back, tickling my skin.

But it's his eyes when he looks at me that affect me the most. Like the breath is being sucked out of my lungs and the memory is being permanently imprinted on my brain. The bar is set for how a man should look at me when he's touching me.

"Are you cold?" he asks when I shiver. He's smoothing my hair over my shoulders. It's wavy again today. Because it's Monday—and because he said he liked it that way.

"No." I shake my head back and forth. "I'm good."

Then he dips his head to my breast and I'm anything but good. Frenzied would be a better word.

"Frenzied?" Vince questions. He asks it with a smirk, his lips a centimeter from my nipple. He's cupping one breast in his hand while playing with the other with his teeth. Did I say 'frenzied' out loud? Jesus, what is even happening right now?

"'Frenzied' is a word that means 'wildly excited,'" I gasp around a wet swipe of his tongue.

"I'm aware."

His lips wrap around my nipple and my back arches as a groan leaves my mouth. His lips, oh, his lips. The scruff of his chin is abrading my sensitive skin, but then his lips are so soft and wet and perfect. The contrast is driving me mad but I never want it to stop. His tongue flicks against my nipple again and I'm wet and hot and needy, as if that tongue is working directly on my clit. I want to rub myself against him, I need to rub myself against him, but I can't. Not in this position, with my legs spread over his, knees on the couch. I try though—I flex my hips, but with his lips wrapped around my tit I can't sink low enough to grind myself against him.

It feels like every part of my body is thrumming and demanding attention. It feels like anywhere he touches me results in one long pang in my core. My earlobe, my elbow, it doesn't matter. It all results in the same throb between my thighs. The desire to be filled and fucked by this man.

Then he moves, shifting me until I'm no longer astride him as he stands. Lifting me from the couch and carrying me to my bedroom. Laying me on my bed before sliding my pajama pants over my hips, past my knees and off my legs. I flex my toes while I watch him undress. He watches me watching him. His shoes come off first. They land on my bedroom floor with a satisfying thump, followed by his socks. I like seeing him like this, tieless, shirt askew, barefoot. This state of semi-undress is strangely erotic to me, but maybe it's just Vince. Because I find him to be quite rousing in every state of dress that I've seen him.

Buckle, zipper, pants.

Buttons, shirt, boxers.

Finally.

The trail of condoms from yesterday are still lying on my dresser. He tosses one onto the bed then climbs over me. His cock weighs heavy on my stomach as he brackets my head with his hands. Then his lips are pressing against mine again. Soft perfect kisses, on my lips and the corners of my mouth. I snake a hand between us and wrap my fingers around him in a caress, an easy slide up and down the length of him, my thumb rubbing over the crown when I reach it, smoothing the pre-cum in a circular motion across the wide tip.

"I want to tell you something." I say it softly, like a whisper because he's so close, because it's what the moment calls for.

"What's that?" His eyes meet mine, flickering across my face as if he can read my thoughts simply by looking at me.

"I know we just met but"—I pause and take a breath—"I like you."

He huffs the tiniest breath of air, like a whispered laugh. The lines around his eyes crinkle and his lips turn into the barest hint of a smile.

"I know."

He kisses me again.

"You've been fairly obvious about it," he adds with another press of his lips.

"It's one of my best qualities," I say. "I'm outgoing. I'm also spontaneous, but I'm not sure if that's a strength or a weakness because it conflicts with both my decision-making and long-term planning skills, which are definitely weaknesses."

He smiles wider this time. Another kiss. "It just so happens that I'm an excellent decision-maker and my long-term planning skills are top-notch."

"You'd be surprised by how much you might have in common with someone completely opposite from you," I offer.

"You've been a non-stop surprise, I'd agree."

"Opposites attract," I whisper.

"Payton." He murmurs the word against my ear, his nose skimming the line of my jaw, his knee pushing between my own.

"Yes?"

"I like you too." Then he kisses the side of my neck and rolls us over so I'm on top. "Straddle me," he directs, tapping my thigh with his hand.

I grin, sitting up and sliding my knees up to bracket his hips. "I'm very flexible. It's one of my strengths. Literally and physically."

"Noted." Vince rips open the condom and sheaths himself as I raise myself over him just enough for him to line us up and then I sink down.

Slowly, one inch at a time as I adjust to the stretch and the feeling of fullness. The depth and angle of the penetration. Vince's eyes are glued to the spot where I'm stretched wide and he's inside of me.

The staring makes me wetter.

He runs his palms up and down the tops of my

thighs as I rise up and down on top of him. I don't rock back and forth, so I'm not getting any friction on my clit, but I don't care because the sensation of being filled by him is the sum total of everything I want in life at this moment. I squeeze my muscles around him as I rise up on my knees, feeling every inch of the drag of his cock inside of me. Then I relax and sink down.

Repeat.

Repeat.

Repeat.

He watches himself disappearing inside of me while I watch him watching us. I clench and he groans. Then he wraps his hands around my wrists and pulls them behind my back. The movement forces my chest forward and I tighten reflexively on his cock as he shifts one hand to contain both my wrists. I could shrug out of this hold if I wanted to, but I don't. I like it. I like that I'm on top but he's in charge. I like the pressure of his fingers against my skin and the angle of his cock in my pussy as I'm forced to lean just slightly back.

Then he moves his free hand to my clit and I like it a lot. Oh, so very much. I think he likes it too because he groans, "God, you're beautiful," as I bounce on top of him while his thumb works me to perfection and I feel beautiful. I feel like I've never been more beautiful to any man, ever. I feel like whatever series of events led my path to cross with Vince's was meant to be, unavoidable, universally predetermined. My head falls back, my neck arched, and I come hard and fast and without warning. The stimulation is too much, too overwhelming, too perfect.

Vince releases my hands and draws me down to

his chest, his hands running soothingly across my back. He has nice hands, I think absently. Big, strong. Good at both restraining and caressing. Cooking and game boards. Fingering and pinching and twisting.

"I like you more than I should," he murmurs into my ear when I'm spread out on top of him. He's still hard inside of me while I'm a puddle of warmth and bliss. I pick my head up off his chest and kiss him, the movement rubbing my nipples against his skin, the contact making me want more. I rock on top of him, my lips pressed against his as I flex my hips and move with him. Then he rolls us so he's on top, but keeps his legs bracketing mine instead of sliding between. He's still inside of me, and it feels different like this, the penetration tighter. I'm again slightly restrained by the position and when he weaves his hands with mine and thrusts all I can do is moan in pleasure and enjoy the feel of him pressed on top of me, inside of me. Vince dips his forehead to mine, his breath heavy and his eyes intense. Our arms are aligned from elbow to fingertips, pressed into the mattress beside my head as his hips flex with purpose and strength.

"I wanted to fuck you like this from behind, but I like looking at you too much."

"It's okay, we can save it for when you think I'm annoying."

He smiles, a quick flash of teeth and slight curve of his lips as his eyes flit across my face. Then he kisses me and thrusts. Hard and deep and perfect. Over and over till I'm nearly incoherent from wanting to come again. So close, so close, so close. When I arch my neck and tighten around him he dips his head into my neck and thrusts hard twice more before stilling over me with a grunt and whispered words about how good I feel, how great I make him feel. I slide my hands out from under his and wrap my arms around his neck because I want as much of his skin touching as much of mine as is possible. Because I want him closer. Because I like him a lot.

Vince kisses my collarbone up the side of my neck and ends with sucking my earlobe between his teeth, which tickles and turns me on at the same time. Then he holds my head between his hands and kisses me before balancing on one elbow and reaching between us to wrap his hand around the base of the condom as he pulls out.

I don't think I've ever given any thought to this moment before. I don't think this act has ever felt so intimate before though, more intimate than entering me in the first place. This post-coital withdrawal from my body, the condom filled with his release and coated in mine. The kissing and the way he watches me as he withdraws.

After he's disposed of the condom he comes back, sliding the covers from beneath me until I lift my bottom and slip my feet under the sheet. I think he's going to tuck me in and leave but instead he slides in beside me.

"A or B," he murmurs as he plays with my hair. I'm tucked into his side, my head and hand on his chest. "A, cats, B, dogs."

"C, both," I answer.

He exhales and I know he's smiling. I can feel it just in the way he breathed. It makes me smile too and I laugh.

"A, chocolate or B, strawberry?"

"That's also a C. Strawberries dipped in

chocolate."

"What if it's a milkshake?"

"Strawberry."

"What if it's pie?"

"Chocolate."

"Ice cream?"

"Chocolate."

"A donut?"

"Strawberry."

"You are wildly inconsistent."

"Maybe." I shrug. "Or maybe I just know what I like."

"Hmm," Vince murmurs. He's still playing with my hair and it feels heavenly, but it's making me so sleepy that I nod off a few questions later.

TWENTY

"I HAVE TO GO, beautiful."

It's early. It's early and Vince is leaning over me in bed, pants on and partially zipped. Shirt hanging loosely open. He presses a kiss to my forehead and repeats the thing about leaving. I take in the light level in the room and determine it's earlier than my alarm, before seven.

"Why?" I yawn.

"I have to be in court at ten and I need to drive home and change first."

Court?

Court!

This is my chance! My chance to prove what a supportive and loyal wife I could be. My chance to contribute! I sit straight up in bed, gathering the sheet to my chest.

"Why? Did you get arrested?" I blink back the sleep and focus on my math-ing. "Do you need bail money? Listen, Vince. I've got about fourteen hundred dollars in a savings account and if I eat all my meals in the employee cafeteria until payday, I could pull another hundred from checking. So if they set your bail at fifteen hundred or under, I'm here for you." I smile, pleased with myself.

Vince looks less pleased. A bit confused. Possibly

alarmed.

Oh, God. It's serious. It's something serious. That's why he married me. I knew it was too good to be true. He's not stupid, he couldn't have been that drunk, I sorta thought he wasn't. I'd assumed it was temporary insanity or just a really, really long time since he'd been laid but maybe what he really wanted was a bride before he got sent away.

"If it's more than that, or if you get convicted, I could wait for you. On the outside," I add when he does nothing but button his shirt and stare at me. "What are we talking here? Five to ten? I'm only twenty-two so we'd still have loads of time." I gather a lock of hair around my fingertip and twist it, because he's not saying anything. "Ten to twenty?" I ask, and I know I must sound slightly less enthusiastic. "Do you think you'll get conjugal visits? Because I'd like to have kids at some point and if we wait until I'm forty that might be pushing it."

He tilts his head to the side, tucking his shirt into his pants and fastening the belt, eyes still on mine, which reminds me of something else. Something besides how cute those kids would be, but I have to focus right now.

"Do you have any dry cleaning that needs to be picked up?" I'm all enthusiasm again, because this I can do. "They don't hold that stuff for more than six months, but I'd be happy to take care of it for you. But only while you're on the inside, we're not going to turn that into a habit." Hot damn, I might even make myself a wife badge because I am nailing this.

"I have to be in court at ten, Payton, because I'm a criminal defense attorney and I'm in the middle of a trial."

Oh. I scrunch my nose. I didn't see that coming, I

really didn't. I was sorta hoping he needed a green card or something, but last night he mentioned he was born in Nevada so that doesn't even make any sense.

"You're a lawyer?" I'm pretty sure that comes out with the kind of tone one reserves for finding out it's going to rain on their wedding day.

"Yes, sorry to disappoint you."

"It's okay." I shrug. "We can still play conjugal prison visit if you want. I could dress up like a sexy prison warden and get furry handcuffs."

Vince shakes his head and mutters something about me being insane.

"Are you a good lawyer?"

"Yes." He smirks, looking amused by my question. "Very good."

Oh. I frown and scratch a dry spot on my arm.

"How long have you been lawyering?"

He smiles at my question, or perhaps my usage of the English language. "Twelve years."

I nod. Wait one second...

"How old are you?" I stare at him as if I've just developed the ability to accurately guess someone's age. I thought he was thirty. Ish? Thirty-two, something like that. But college plus law school plus twelve years equals something more than thirty-two.

"Thirty-seven."

"Stop it!" I know my eyes are wide. "You're old. Older. Older than I thought, is what I mean." I wrinkle my nose as I look him over again. I really thought he was younger. I wonder how I feel about this? It makes me feel a little hot for teacher if I'm being honest with myself. Which I always am. Honest with myself, that is. Like right now, I'm going to add why this turns me on to my list of things that may or may not be wrong with me.

He laughs at me. Flat-out laughs at me. As if my complete disregard for fact-checking amuses him.

"You should learn to ask a few questions before you elope with someone, Payton."

"Yeah well, you really shouldn't have married me without a prenup. That sounds like a pretty rookie move for a very good lawyer. With so much experience." I side-eye him when I say it. Except that I'm looking straight at him so it's more of an eye roll.

"Watch it, or I'll take you for half of that fifteen hundred dollars you've got."

"That's fine." I shrug. "Because I'm going to need my cut of your club. We've only been married for a couple days though and I pride myself on my reasonableness so I'll settle for a month's worth of free drinks."

"You pride yourself on your reasonableness? Did those words just leave your mouth?"

"I'm extremely reasonable! Everyone says so!"

"No one says that."

"You have no idea if that's true."

Vince exhales and shakes his head. "Never do your own negotiating. I just took half your net worth and all you want is a month of free drinks?"

"Did I aim too low? Can I get free nachos too?"

"You're nuts."

"Says you, wait until you see my student loan debt."

"Student loan debt obtained before a marriage is not transferrable to the spouse in the event of separation in Nevada."

"Well, that sucks." I sigh dramatically. "Do you work at a fancy practice? Do lawyers call it a practice or is that only doctors? Are you the boss? Do you have a good benefits package?" I cross my legs under the sheets and rest my elbows on my knees.

"I have my own firm so yes, I work for myself and yes, I'm the boss. And yes, I offer a comprehensive benefits package to all employees."

Comprehensive. I try not to roll my eyes. He *really* didn't need my health insurance.

"I guess all that legal knowledge will come in handy for annulling me."

"I think you're improperly using 'annulling.'"

"Yeah, like English language rules have ever slowed me down before." I shrug mulishly. "I'm not paying for half of the annulment, so don't even think about billing me. It probably took you eight minutes to fill out that paperwork and you'll bill me for fifteen minutes at some ridiculous rate of two hundred an hour."

"Seven hundred."

"What?"

"I bill at seven hundred an hour."

I stare at him, trying to compute that, but that kind of math-ing is meant for a calculator.

"I have to go, I'll see you later."

"I don't understand. What kind of lawyer who makes that kind of money owns a gentlemen's club? What kind of a lawyer owns a gentlemen's club period? Oh! Is it because of your mom? Did she used to work there? Do you have some kind of emotional attachment to the place?"

He bends his neck like I'm possibly asking too many questions for this early in the morning, or ever. He rests a hand on my doorframe, already halfway out the door.

"It's complicated." He ruffles a hand through his

hair and I wonder if this is a thing he does when he's thinking about things he doesn't want to talk about. "It's more of a hobby thing."

I nod. Most guys play golf, or join a fantasy football league, but it's fine. I don't want to be that wife who rolls in and demands he give up his stripper hobby for me.

"A strip club must make a lot of money." What in the hell does he need the money for if he's already making a calculator amount per hour lawyering?

"Good ones do."

"Is yours a good one?"

"No." He shakes his head, seeming amused with my question. "I suppose it's not based on that criteria."

"It's okay, I'm not judging you," I assure him.

"No?"

"I spend a lot of money on my hobbies too." Fuck, I don't have any hobbies.

"Such as?" Of course he'd ask.

"I spend somewhere around eight or ten dollars a week on Cheez-Its."

"Your hobby is eating crackers?"

"I'm also quite crafty. I make dirty Girl Trooper achievement badges for Lydia." Crap, I really do need a hobby. Maybe I can get Lydia to teach me something useful like sewing or crockpot-ing. "Anyway, good talk. Good luck in court today. Break a leg. Bill some hours."

He pauses, a smile on his face as he looks me over one last time. Then he taps he doorframe twice with his hand and leaves. I hear the kitchen chair scrape against the tile as he grabs his suit jacket and then the front door opens and closes.

Damn. Vince is a real conundrum. Usually the

super hot ones aren't this complex. I stare at the empty doorway and think about last night. That was fun, staying in and playing a board game. It was even more fun than our drunken night on Fremont Street. The sex was even better than it was the first time too, and the first time was mind-blowing. It's like every encounter I have with him is better than the last, but I'm a little bit crazy so I'm not sure my feelings can or should be trusted.

I reach over and grab my phone from the nightstand to confirm the time. My alarm won't be sounding for another hour, but there's no chance I'm going back to sleep now. I swipe the alarm to off and tap the side of my phone with my fingers, a bundle of nervous energy. I might as well get ready early. I could run an errand on the way to work. Like stopping at WinCo to pick up some groceries. Nothing perishable since it'll have to sit in my car all day, but I could replenish my Cheez-It supply. I could go to work early and get a head start on my day.

I could review the contents of the envelope that's sitting on my kitchen counter.

I toss the sheets off and get up. I've showered, dressed and applied my make-up in under twenty minutes. Mornings are faster with a bit of adrenaline. I braid my hair on the way to the kitchen to encourage the curls while it air-drys.

The envelope is gone.

I know it was on the countertop last night, I know it was. I cleaned the entire counter, put everything away and wiped down the counter. All that was left was that envelope. I tapped it with my fingers, didn't I? I held it in my hands, just before Vince wanted to play Scrabble. I check the floor, wondering if it somehow fell. I check the trash and the kitchen table and the dishwasher.

It's gone.

What the hell does that mean? Vince wanted me to read them or sign them or something, didn't he? I consider texting him, I do consider it. It'd be the most logical way to proceed, but I like to think outside of the box. Thinking outside of the box is probably what my life coach would tell me to do if I asked her. If she had any idea who I was.

Measure twice and cut once is what a carpenter would tell me, which is completely irrelevant to the issue at hand, but it's a nice sentiment, isn't it? It's a nice way of saying, *Do your research*. Which, now that I think of it like that, makes it totally relevant. Plan and prepare in a thorough manner before taking action.

I know just what to do.

TWENTY—ONE

"SO THEN HE'S all 'it's more of a hobby,' and I'm not the hobby police, right? I'm not that girl. I'm very reasonable, in case you didn't know that about me. It's true. People say it." I pause there and hold up a hand in a very casual stop gesture. "Maybe not a lot of people, but it's been said at least a couple of times."

"I can only imagine."

"But then I thought, maybe he has other hobbies. Maybe he builds model trains or plays softball. I've seen him naked so softball is much more likely than model train-building, but I don't know for sure do I? Maybe it's golf or running that he's into. I know he's a good cook, but is that a hobby or a chore? I'm his wife and I should know these things, take an interest in his interests. Do a little research so I can impress him with my knowledge."

"Payton?"

"Wait! One other thing. Then he took the envelope with him! When he left the envelope was gone. Like what does that even mean?"

"Payton."

"Yes?"

"Why in the hell are you in my officer telling me all of this? And why did you"—Lawson glances down and back to me—"put a dollar in change on my desk?"

"Oh, that's your retainer. I didn't have any singles. You can count it though, it's all there."

"My retainer?"

"Yeah. So you can tell me everything you know about Vince, because now we have attorney-client privilege."

"That's not what a retainer is for. Nor how attorney-client privilege works," Lawson replies with a slow shake of his head and an expression that indicates he thinks I'm very, very incorrect.

"But you're a lawyer."

"I am."

We stare at each other for a moment.

"And now I'm your client." I nod towards the pile of change on his desk.

"Nope." Lawson shakes his head back and forth. "First of all, I'm a corporate lawyer, and I'm employed by the Windsor so I don't take on clients. Secondly, I believe you're under the misapprehension that attorney-client privilege means I'd tell you everything I know about Vince."

"Right! And I won't tell him anything you said. Because we have the privilege!"

"Lastly, what you need for your annulment is a family law attorney."

I slump in the chair across from Lawson's desk. "So you think he's going to annul me? I was hoping he'd changed his mind when he left with the paperwork."

"Payton, I have no idea what's going on between the two of you and I don't know Vince well enough to guess. If it helps any, I don't think he can serve you with annulment paperwork himself so maybe he wanted to go over it with you so you'd know what to expect."

"Yeah, okay." I sigh as I stand up. "Thanks anyway. You're fired." I get the first real smile of the day out of Lawson as I swipe the pile of change off his desk and into my palm.

"Canon golfs with him. He'd know more and that fucker loves to gossip."

"Thanks. By the way, did your parents name you Lawson because they hoped you'd become a lawyer?"

"It's my mother's maiden name."

"Oh." I nod. "I suppose that makes more sense."

"A little bit." He nods. "Good luck, Payton."

TWENTY–TWO

ON THURSDAY VINCE texts because he has a late meeting. He texts because he's been over every night but tonight he has to work late. It's downright domestic, right? The way he checks in. The way he shows up every night after I arrive home from work, arriving with a bag of groceries or takeout. We cook and eat and play games. Then we fuck like rabbits and he spends the night. It's domestic anarchy. I think? A domestic revolution? It's playing house while ignoring the elephant in the room, is what it is.

So on Thursday he texts first telling me he's got a late meeting and asking if he should still come over, or if I want to eat without him. Of course I still want him to come over. I even volunteer to make dinner, like some kind of housewife. By housewife I mean a shitty one, not a Lydia one. I don't have chicken-roasting skills in my wheelhouse. I make scrambled eggs and cinnamon French toast because other than opening boxes of Cheez-Its, it's my specialty, but Vince doesn't seem to care. Instead he thanks me. Then we eat breakfast for dinner at nine PM before playing a children's board game because it's the only game in the stack we haven't played yet.

The envelope doesn't make another appearance. I start to wonder if it was ever real to begin with, if I ever saw it at all. Maybe it was just a figment of my overactive imagination? Or maybe hoping I never saw it is the delusion? I know the wedding really happened because I have this gold band on my finger to remind me, same as Vince, because we're both still wearing them.

I could ask him what exactly our status is, as a couple. I know I could ask. I know I should ask. But the thing is, this marriage is still very new. So I don't want to remind him that we're married by asking about the marriage. You know? Fine, you probably don't know, but it's a really tricky situation and I'm not a marriage expert. It's not as though you'd ask a guy you'd been dating a week what his intentions were. I just happened to marry a guy and then date him for a week after the wedding. By 'just happen' I mean a drunken elopement that is no more than seventy percent my fault. Fine, eighty. Eighty-five percent, max.

Maybe you'd know better how to handle it, if it happened to you. Maybe you'd never get yourself in such a situation to begin with. I get it—I have a lot of opinions on things too—but I'm not an expert on anything. I'm not even an expert on being me, but I'm trying. I'm trying to be the best me I can be. I'm trying to make the best of this incredibly bizarre situation I'm in and work out my feelings for Vince at the same time. Live my best life and all that.

On Saturday morning Vince gets up before I do, per the routine that's been set all week. Except it's Saturday, so it kinda sucks and catches me a bit off guard. He told me he had work to do, kissed me on my forehead and left. I was half asleep due to an early-morning round of sex so I didn't protest. It didn't even occur to me that it was Saturday until I awoke some time later and realized I had nowhere to be.

And that I had no plans with Vince for the weekend. Or in general, really.

I wonder where he's at. The club? His law office? I don't even know where his law office is. Downtown, he said, when I asked if he ran the law firm from the club. He laughed. I suppose the idea of a bunch of lawyers working out of a gentlemen's club is rather ridiculous.

It occurs to me that I wanted to take more of an interest in his hobbies. Just last night he watched the new episode of *Married at First Sight* with me because I told him it was my hobby. Which is true—it's sort of a hobby, right? Watching reality television? It is for me, I decide, and I don't think anyone should judge anyone else's hobbies. Besides, I find it both relaxing and informative so it's more of an educational hobby.

In any case, I should take an interest in Vince's hobbies. It'd be so wifely of me.

As luck would have it, I have just the idea.

TWENTY-THREE

"OKAY, WHERE DO I start?" I eye the pole and take a test swing around. By swing I mean both my feet are firmly on the floor, one hand on the pole, and I let the momentum of my upper body swing me around.

"Well, you can start by taking off the stripper heels. If you break your ankle Vince is going to kill me."

"They're just my regular fuck-me heels. Stripper heels seems offensive, no?"

"Just take them off."

I sigh and kick my heels off, pushing them out of the way with my toe.

"We don't even offer dance classes, but you're oddly convincing." Staci frowns like she's not sure how she's found herself here. We're on the main floor of Double Diamonds in a sort of side room. It's off the main entrance, but it was empty and the lights dimmed, kinda like a section in a restaurant that hasn't been assigned a waitress. There are two poles on this stage and it's a little bit quieter in here because we've turned the speakers off—the music from the main stage is more than loud enough to reach us, but this way we can talk. "Are you sure Vince said this was okay? I don't want to lose my scholarship."

Err. Technically what I told her is that Vince wouldn't mind. I don't think I said he said it was okay. When I said he wouldn't mind I meant that as my impression of what Vince's feelings would be, not an actual conversation.

"That's a positive attribute, don't you think? Being convincing?"

"Sure?" Staci shrugs like she's completely indifferent to the value of a convincing argument. Or the ability to get someone to teach you how to pole-dance.

I wonder why she called her job a scholarship? Is it some kind of bullshit strip club lingo? I should know the lingo.

"Why did you say 'scholarship?' Is that some kind of word that means 'job?'"

"No." Staci glances over at me like I'm the one not making any sense. "I'm in law school at UNLV. On a club scholarship."

Right. A club scholarship. I'm about to ask what the hell that means when Staci's attention is diverted.

"We're in training," Staci says to a guy who attempts to come in and watch. I smile and wave because I appreciate the support. If I was actually trying to earn money as a dancer it's good to know I have tip-earning potential. Plus I'm in workout shorts and a sports bra, my hair in a ponytail, so it's not exactly like I'm putting forth a real effort here.

"Who comes to a gentlemen's club at eleven in the morning?" I ask Staci once the guy has left.

"Guys who work overnights, usually. Sometimes retirees. Lonely people, mostly. The world is filled with lonely people, Payton, just looking for a little human interaction wherever they can get it. I've got a weekday regular who comes in, drinks coffee and reads the paper. Says he likes the chairs." Staci shrugs again.

"Oh. That's sad."

"Some of them are just regular perverts, if it makes you feel better."

"It does a little."

"Let's focus," Staci says, directing my attention back to the task at hand. "First thing you want to do is sanitize your pole. They're cleaned between each dancer and every night, but it's a good habit to learn." Staci squirts her pole with a bottle of spray sanitizer before handing it to me along with a clean towel. I'm still doing my best not to laugh at 'sanitize your pole,' but I do my best to keep my giggles in check and follow instructions.

"Next, we stretch. Normally you'd do this backstage, obviously."

"Obviously." I nod along as Staci leads me through a series of warm-up stretches. "Is this a club policy?"

"No, it's common sense."

"Sure, that makes sense too."

"Okay, now which is your dominant hand?"

"My right."

"Good, me too, so you can mirror what I'm doing. We'll start with a basic wrap-around. I'll show you once then we'll go through it step by step." Staci grabs the pole with one hand and swings, hooking the pole with one leg as her body rotates. Back arched, she completes a few rotations on the pole before straightening, her foot returning to the floor, hand still on the pole as her momentum comes to a stop. "Easy," she says. "Now I'll show you step by step."

It's a lot easier than it looks. A whole lot. I'm on my third attempt when we're interrupted by another wannabe customer. I figure Staci will direct them to the main stage as I twirl badly around the pole, but when I come to a stop I realize why she's not saying anything.

It's Vince.

He doesn't look impressed.

"No."

That's all he says. No. He doesn't even blink but a muscle in his jaw most definitely twitches. It's enough to send Staci on her way, Vince not breaking eye contact with me as she exits. It's a small stage, elevated only a few feet off the floor, but I still have the height advantage over Vince. I place a hand on my hip and toss the other in the air in a gesture meant to imply 'what the fuck.'

"I'm taking an interest in your hobbies," I explain, because clearly he's not understanding the effort I'm making here.

"Get down."

"Get down? I'm not a cat."

"Payton," he starts then stops, squeezing his eyes shut for a moment and rubbing his forehead with his hand. I wonder if he's about to tell me he's going to count to three? I'd be totally into that. "Please get down," is what he says when he opens his eyes again. It's a bit of a letdown to be honest.

I didn't come here to pick a fight so I grab my heels and step off of the platform, stopping directly in front of him. I drop my heels on the floor and then use Vince for balance as I slip them on one at a time, smiling at him when I'm done.

"Staci wasn't busy, she said it doesn't pick up until

after lunch. It's just retirees and newspapers until then so I wasn't really distracting her." I bite my lip, wondering if I should reimburse her for lost tips. I should, I decide. "Also I told her it was okay with you, so don't be mad at her. It's not her fault."

"My office," he instructs as he turns, holding an arm out to indicate I should walk in front of him.

I do, following the path I recall from the week prior. It's so loud in the main room of the club that I can't hear my heels click against the floor, or Vince's footsteps behind me, but I know he's there because I can feel him hovering directly behind me.

Vince closes his office door behind us as I plop onto the same chair I sat in last week, sitting across from his desk. I cross my legs and arms, prepared to defend my right to learn how to pole-dance, but Vince surprises me by not sitting. He stops at my chair and places his hands on the arms of the chair, leaning down until we're inches apart.

"What would possess you to show up here half naked and think I'd be okay with it?" He says it softly, his voice gravelly and seductive.

"I told you, I was taking an interest in your hobbies." My own voice is much less confident in my reply. Less confident in my plan than I previously was.

"Payton, you cannot be here dressed like that."

"Why not? Everyone else is." Excellent opening argument, if I do say so myself.

"I'm not married to everyone else," He looks surprised that he mentioned it, the marriage. I do enjoy the reminder that he's aware that we're married. Also, it really seems to bring out the alpha male bullshit in him, which I love—as long as I still get to do whatever I want, obviously.

"It's our one-week anniversary," I point out. I mean it as a joke, sort of. Since he brought it up. But I realize it's true, it's been one week since I sat in this exact chair. One week since we got married. A week in which we've spent every day together—every evening, in any case. Which is basically like having seven dates.

Which is irrelevant because no one gets married after seven dates. Except for the couples on those reality shows I love about strangers marrying each other. Or arranged marriages, I bet they don't date much beforehand. There'd be no point really, since it's already arranged. And we all know those marriages have a higher rate of success than the average bozos who get to know each other first.

It's been fun getting to know him though. Really fun. The board games and the cooking and the talking. The sleepovers and the chatting until we fall asleep. Learning what we have in common, and what we don't. But maybe he doesn't want more. Maybe I'm the only one interested in moving this from accidental to purposeful.

"About that." He rises now, stepping back and putting distance between us, sitting on the edge of his desk, his hands bracketing the desk on either side of his hips. He glances away for a moment and I wonder if he's finally going to bring up the annulment paperwork again.

For the record, I'm not bringing it up. Like, ever. Unless it's our twenty-fifth wedding anniversary and the statute of limitations on annulments has run out. Wait, I don't think there is a statute of limitations on annulments. I think that term is meant for crimes, or tax evasion. But whatever, I'm not bringing it up, is the point.

Vince locks eyes with me again for a long moment before letting out a small huff of breath. Then shakes his head a little and smiles.

"Pole dancing is the traditional one-week gift?"

"No. Pole dancing was me taking an interest in your hobbies."

"Right. I forgot. My hobbies."

"So I can't learn to pole-dance?"

"Not here, you can't." He crosses his arms and stares me down. "Though obviously I can't tell you what you can or can't do, Payton."

"No, you can't." Glad we're on the same page about that. Seriously, I am ridiculously good at picking husbands. I wonder if I should start a matchmaking business? That would be the ultimate event planning position, wouldn't it? It'd be like life planning. Oh, my God. I'd be like a life coach. A matchmaking life coach! I really hope I remember this idea later. I lose some really great ideas because I forget to write them down.

"I hope you brought some clothing to wear out of here because you're not wearing that."

"I'm wearing twice as much material as I wear at the pool," I argue. I wonder if I have untapped lawyer potential? I decide it doesn't matter because I'd much rather plan events than argue with anyone. Plus the matchmaking life coaching thing is a much better idea.

"Then you need a new swimsuit," Vince retorts. "Or a private pool."

I roll my eyes. "Listen, Vince. Good news. I have a backup plan for today."

"I legiterally cannot wait to hear it."

TWENTY-FOUR

"WE'RE"—HE PAUSES with a look around us—"mini-golfing?"

"Yes!" I nearly bounce with excitement because this was a very good idea. "Because you like golf! And I don't know how to golf, but I'm an excellent mini-golfer. And you can work on your putting! Great idea, right?"

"With glow-in-the-dark golf balls." Vince is looking around the place like he's entered the Twilight Zone. Which he sorta has because I've brought him to the Twilight Zone indoor mini-golf course at Bally's. The entire place is glow in the dark and themed around the *Twilight Zone* movie.

"Yeah. Is that gonna throw off your game, big guy? Are you already looking for an excuse for losing?"

"Oh, I'm not losing."

"Says you. I'm an excellent mini-golfer."

We find the admission booth and pay—well, Vince pays. I attempted to, but he insisted and since I calculator-mathed that seven-hundred-dollar-an-hour billing rate of his I didn't fight him on it. I pick out a glow-in-the-dark pink ball for myself and ask him if he'd like a blue ball. Then I laugh like a twelve-year-old because honestly, does anyone ever outgrow ball jokes? I hope not.

"I'll keep score," I announce and grab a tiny scorecard and pencil. I write our names on the scorecard as Vince slides his credit card back into his wallet. I like the way our names look together. Payton and Vince. Like a team, even though we're competing against each other, being on the same score card makes us a sort of unit. In my mind at least, and I'm keeping this card forever. I'll tuck it into a drawer somewhere or maybe put it between the pages of a book like a pressed flower. Which reminds me...

"I like to read!" I announce out of nowhere. I drop my ball in the tee box area at hole one. I wonder if there's an official term for this or if tee box is it.

"That's good to hear," Vince deadpans.

I smile, because my outburst was pretty random. I like the way he rolls with my randomness.

"As a hobby. I like to read books as a hobby."

"That's an excellent hobby."

"I didn't think of it the other day when you asked me what my hobbies were. And I wanted you to know I have a hobby other than eating Cheez-Its."

"So I should cancel the case of Cheez-Its in custom-made boxes I've got on order?"

I blink and side-eye him, not sure if he's joking or not. I give it a full three seconds of thought before accepting it's a joke because I don't think anyone offers custom Cheez-It boxes, but who wouldn't want that to be real? I stick out my tongue at him and take my shot. The ball stops half a foot from the hole.

"What kind of books do you like to read?"

"Romance novels." I say it proudly because I don't care if he is a fancy lawyer, I'm not embarrassed about my choice of reading material. Besides, you wouldn't believe the number of romance authors who used to practice law but stopped because practicing law was dreadful. I wonder if Vince thinks practicing law is dreadful? Maybe that's why he owns the club? Because he needs fulfillment outside of work? "Do you hate lawyering?"

"I thought we were talking about reading?" Vince takes his shot, his ball stopping a few inches from mine.

"We were, I got distracted."

"I love lawyering. I usually refer to it as practicing the law, but lawyering is catchier. I think I'll send a memo on Monday and ask everyone at the firm to refer to their jobs as lawyering from now on."

"You really should."

We both finish hole one in two strokes and move on to the next hole. There's a family a few holes ahead of us, so we take our time, knowing we're going to eventually catch up as we'll move faster as a party of two than they will with a party of four.

"What do you love about it?" I ask.

"I like solving problems. I like helping people who need my help. I like making a difference."

"But you're in criminal law, right? So sometimes you have to help criminals?"

"Sometimes, yeah. That's how the law works. Sometimes the clients are innocent. Sometimes they're not. Most of the time they're just people who made bad choices and need help working through their options."

"What else do you like about it?"

"I like owning my own firm. I like working for myself, essentially. Being the boss. Taking on the cases that interest me. I like that it affords me the opportunity to do what I want."

Vince pauses to take his shot. He's wearing a white shirt, which glows in this light. I've never mini-golfed indoors before, but I decide this is fun. Or maybe it's being with Vince that makes it fun.

"What do you like about event planning?"

"Oh, you know, all those same things," I joke. I hit my ball and it bounces off the side wall and rolls straight into the hole. "Hole in one!" I do a little shimmy to celebrate. Vince laughs, the lines around his eyes creasing. I love those little lines, they drive me absolutely nuts. He's got one on his forehead too, this perfect line he gets when he's deep in thought. I usually see it when I've said something ridiculous. It comes out before the long pause while he considers whatever it is that I've said.

"Nice. Now tell me what you like about your job."

"I like helping people socialize. I really do. Which is weird maybe, but it's not easy for everyone. Like Lydia, she's not as outgoing as I am. She'd never have met Rhys if I hadn't dragged her out of the house. She'd have stayed home and made sheet pajamas until she was thirty. Also, I sorta like the budgeting aspect."

"How so?"

"It's kinda like a puzzle. I have a budget and a head count and a general ideas of what the client is interested in. And then I present a bunch of options, like a giant game of A or B, and help them piece together the best version of their event. It's fun."

"You plan a lot of weddings, right?"

"For now." I bristle. "But I'm working on a very exciting dermatology event."

"You don't like working on the weddings?" Vince seems surprised by this fact and it sorta pisses me off.

"Just because I'm a girl doesn't mean I've spent my entire life obsessing about weddings."

"No," he replies slowly. "I hadn't meant to imply as such."

"I am an event planner"—I stress the word 'event'—"who happens to plan weddings when they're assigned to me."

"Got it. You're not a wedding girl. Maybe you can convince your wedding customers to elope like you did."

"That'd probably get me fired," I reply, wondering if the elopement thing was a dig.

"Quite the moral dilemma you find yourself in."

"It's a real pickle, Vince. A real deep-fried pickle."

He laughs and then I say more than I intended to. "I wish I could convince my mother to elope."

"You don't like the guy she's marrying?"

"He's fine, I guess. I don't really know him, I was in already in college when they met, so..." I shrug. "He's her fourth husband so I'm not sure how seriously I'm supposed to take the whole thing. I'm not buying a monogrammed gift, I know that much."

Vince is looking at me thoughtfully and it makes me uncomfortable. Like he's trying to piece together the psyche of a girl who might have long-term commitment issues, hates weddings but likes eloping, and he isn't sure if it all adds up to anything sane.

We're on the sixth hole when I get a great idea. I'm leading by four so it's an especially good idea for me.

"Hey! I know what we need to do."

"What's that?"

"Raise the stakes."

"Raise the stakes?"

"Yup." I grin.

"Sure. How can we do that? How can we possibly raise the bar on this insanity? Do you want to borrow someone's baby this weekend to test if we'd be good parents?"

I stop dead in my tracks because that's a much better idea than the one I had.

"Wait, it that a real thing that we could do? Do you know someone?"

Vince is staring back at me with a very odd expression on his face and I realize he was kidding. Like super kidding.

"I was kidding, Payton. You can't test-drive a baby, Jesus. How much more insane can any of this get?"

"I know that! I was kidding too. Haha."

He stares.

"Anyway, while the baby-sampling sounds like a great idea, I had something else in mind."

"Baby-sampling," he mutters to himself like I'm the crazy person who brought it up to begin with. That was him, to be clear. In case anyone forgot.

"Whoever wins mini-golf gets to tie the other person up." I wink dramatically so he gets my drift. My drift is sex. Someone's hands tied to the headboard, is what I'm envisioning.

Vince takes his first shot on hole three and then looks me over, head to toe and back again, as if he's mentally undressing me.

"So if I win, I can tie you up?"

"Yes!" I grin big.

"I can do that anyway," he finally says.

This guy. I sigh and resist flipping him off because we're in public and children are present.

"Listen, buzzkill, it's still a real good offer."

"I'm not sure that you understand the concept of negotiating."

"Fine. What do I have that you want?"

"Everything," he replies. His voice is low and husky, the word spoken softly, and he's looking me right in the eye when he says it. The swans in my stomach just found a water park that has water bumper cars. You know the ones? They look like giant inner tubes but they have a seat and they're motorized and you use them to float around the lake banging into each other. My stomach swans are definitely banging. Spinning in circles and banging into everything in their path.

"Okay," I reply, not quite trusting my voice to speak. Wondering if I'm reading too much into this. "If I win, I get to tie you up and if you win, you can have whatever you want."

"Deal." He sticks out his hand so we can shake on it. It's oddly funny yet sexual at the same time. I slip my hand into his and we shake. I've felt his hands in mine and on various parts of my body too many times to count this past week, but it still affects me. The spark. The current between us. He winks and I nearly come on the spot. Well, not really. But I am extremely turned on and needy and would not say no if he wanted to abandon this game of mini-golf right now in favor of a hotel room and some kinky good times.

But I can be patient.

More patient than you'd think a girl who elopes on the first date would be.

So I remain confident in my certain victory for the next three holes, but by the tenth, we're tied again. He pulls ahead on the twelfth. We're tied again on the thirtieth. And then it's all downhill. I lose by eight strokes. But let's face it, this was a win for me either way.

I'm practically vibrating with excitement over what he might want to do tonight, with his win. Butt stuff? Nipple clamps? Fuck without a condom? Film a homemade sex tape?

Confess that he's crazy in love with me?

TWENTY-FIVE

HE WANTS TO HAVE dinner at the Cheesecake Factory.

Yup. The Cheesecake Factory.

On a Saturday night.

His choice.

It took forty-seven minutes to get a table. I counted every one of them.

Then he didn't order cheesecake.

He ordered salmon. With broccoli. No dessert. It was very nearly our first fight.

I had a barbecue chicken pizza without the onions because I still intended to have sex with him even though he purposely picked a restaurant with a long wait for no other reason than to amuse himself at my expense. I also ordered two slices of cheesecake to go. They were both for me.

After dinner things finally started looking up.

"I need to stop at Target," he tells me as he makes a left out of the Cheesecake Factory instead of a right which would bring us back to the Beltway and my apartment.

Fuck, yes.

"Do you need to pick up a few supplies for your win, sir?" I ask it in my best sex kitten voice, running a fingertip up his forearm, my imagination already racing with ideas.

"Exactly." He picks up my hand and kisses my palm before placing my hand onto the console between us, with a smile shot in my direction, then focuses on the road again.

Oh, yeah. Kink city. It's happening.

"Stay here," he instructs as he puts the car into park. "I'll be quick." Another sly grin, with a lingering glance at my lips, and he's gone. The car is still running, and my pulse is racing in overtime.

What could he possibly get in a Target? Nipple clamps are out. Unless he's going to buy a box of binder clips. I cringe at the very idea. That cannot be safe so that's out.

Duct tape? The thing is, I cannot imagine how that wouldn't hurt coming off and I'm not looking for real pain, just a bit of fun pain. Like maybe a light rope burn at worst.

Lube? They sell lube, right?

This is torture. How long has he been gone? I eye the clock on the dashboard, wishing I'd thought to check it when he got out of the car. What's it been? Three minutes? Ten minutes? I've no idea.

Maybe he's decided to take me up on my kinky prison warden offer and he's assembling a sexy prisoner costume for me. I wonder what that would look like? Would he put me in a black bra and panties? Stockings and a garter belt? Or would he put me in a denim shirt, naked underneath and barely covering my ass?

What if he's really just out of toothpaste?

I've never been so horny in my entire life. And by never I mean that I'm tempted to stick my hand down my pants and rub one out in this parking lot. I don't, because it's well lit and I don't want to get arrested for public indecency even if I am married to an excellent criminal defense attorney, but I'm tempted. I do cross my legs really tightly while I wait though.

Twelve minutes. Plus whatever minutes I forgot to count in the beginning.

It's another three minutes before he reappears. I've got my head turned to the side, watching the automatic doors for him to appear, so I spot him the moment the doors swish and he exits, bag in hand.

Except what the hell is in that bag? A shirt box? No...

No way.

I watch him walk towards the car, my eyes trained on that stupid bag. He's not holding it by the skimpy plastic handles, instead the box is sticking out of top of the bag while the entire thing is tucked under his arm. Then he's at the car door. He opens in, bending a bit so he can meet my eyes as he shakes the box and grins before tossing it into the back of the car and sliding behind the wheel.

Monopoly.

He wants to play Monopoly.

What kind of a sick pervert wants to play a board game that takes forever when he's got a hot blonde up for anything? Like, legiterally. Anything.

I turn my head and look at it in the backseat, needing visual confirmation one more time that I didn't imagine this. Nope, I didn't. The bag isn't even lumpy, so there's definitely not a hidden bottle of lube or a rope or even a packet of clothespins. I turn around and face forward while Vince reverses the car out of the parking space and turns us in the direction of my apartment.

He talks the entire way home about how much

he's loving our board game time, and how Monopoly was his favorite growing up, and I feel like a perverted jerk. Maybe all the sexual innuendo was in my head? I was pretty clear, wasn't I? Still, it's nice that he enjoys spending time with me, isn't it? Time in which we're talking and not having sex. *Think of the big picture, Payton. He likes you, really likes you.* He could be doing a lot of other things tonight, but he wants to play Monopoly with me.

That's... nice.

I carry my cheesecake bag into the apartment. Vince carries the bag with his Monopoly game, still talking about our impending epic game night. I stick my cheesecake in the fridge and then pull out a kitchen chair and sit, resting my chin in my hand.

Then Vince pulls a flat package out of the bag, flat enough that I didn't notice it under the board game box. He tears at the flap, the sticker ripping the cardboard sleeve. My curiosity is piqued as he tugs the item free of the packaging.

Stockings.

Okay, wow. Game night just got interesting. He holds them up so they unfurl, twin ribbons of black nylon or spandex or whatever the hell a pair of stockings you can buy at Target are made of.

"You want me to wear those while we play?" My mind races, imagining me naked save for these black thigh-highs. I like where this is going.

"No."

Maybe I don't like where this is going. Is now the time Vince reveals that he's into womenswear? Like, for himself? No hate or anything but I don't think I'm into that. Perhaps I could try though? For Vince?

"Stand up," Vince instructs and I have no idea

what's going on, but I do. I stand, pushing my chair in once I'm up, my hands resting on the chair back as I stare at Vince. Then he laughs. "If you could see your face," he says. I blink, still not sure what's going on.

"Are we playing Monopoly or..." I trail off.

"Take off your shirt."

Or not, it appears. I lift my shirt over my head, draping it over the chair back when it's off.

"Bra."

I remove that too, placing it on top of my shirt. Then I shiver, my nipples at attention in the cool of the apartment air-conditioning and Vince's gaze.

"Come here."

It's not until I'm in front of him and he's spun me around, pushing me chest down onto the kitchen countertop and tying my hands behind my back with the stockings, that I get it. I agree, that took me an embarrassingly long time.

When my hands are secure he kisses his way down my spine as his hands locate the side zipper on the skirt I'm wearing. A moment later it falls to the floor in a soft whoosh, then his thumbs hook into my panties and they follow suit. Then he slaps my ass with an open palm and I jump, but before I can react further he's yanked me upright and is walking me in the direction of my room and I feel so dirty. Good dirty. Fantastically dirty. Seductively dirty.

When I'm in front of my bed he turns me to face him then pushes me back until I'm on my back. My arms are bound, trapped beneath me, and it's not the most comfortable position in the world but it does serve to tilt my pelvis perfectly in his direction. Especially once he's picked my dangling legs up and spread them wide, heels on the edge of the bed, thighs open.

"Don't move."

I won't. It would take a lot of effort to get up with my arms tied behind me and besides, I really like where this is going.

Vince moves to my nightstand, the one with the condom stash and the complimentary packet of lube. Except that's not a condom in his hand. It's my eye mask. The one I sometimes use if I'm sleeping late on a weekend and the outside light is too bright as it peeks around the edges of the mini-blinds covering my window. When he slips it over my eyes my heart rate speeds way up. Darkness ups the ante in a very big way. The reduction of sight heightens every sound in the room, my ears eager to identify his slightest movement and what it might mean for me.

The dresser across from my bed creaks, just barely. I imagine that he's leaned up against it, arms casually crossed while he stares at me spread open on the bed. It's embarrassing, but it's hot.

I hear something, the slightest movement a moment before he runs his fingertip down the inside of my thigh. I jump, my legs coming together out of instinct.

"I said not to move. Do I need to tie your legs open, Payton?"

"No." I shake my head in denial, but I'm not sure why I'm saying no because the idea of him tying my legs open has made me so wet I'm sure he can see it for himself. "I'll be good." Maybe. "Goodish," I qualify because I don't want to mislead him. Then I let my legs fall open and arch my feet in nervous anticipation. Or is it excited anticipation? Both, most likely. Being restrained makes me feel like his. I wonder if that's weird or messed up, but I feel it just the same. Like I can let go of all the stress of not knowing where this relationship is going. Because while my hands are tied, it's all on him to make me feel good and safe and wanted. There's nothing I can do but accept it, enjoy it. Revel in his touch and attention.

Vince laughs, a low breathy exhale. Then he taps my clit with his fingertip and there's absolutely no possibility of me holding still. It's so much more intense when I can't see what he's doing. I'm jumpy and wound up and I'm sure I've never been this turned on in my life. Vince is between my legs so I can't do more than squeeze my thighs around him. When his tongue flicks over my clit I'm willing to admit I've been too hasty in my analysis of how turned on I am because the bar of my arousal keeps getting raised.

"Please let me come," I beg.

"You want to come?" Vince's voice is amused. "You want to come three minutes into this game?"

"Yes, please!" Has it really only been three minutes? "Then we can play Monopoly. Or whatever you want."

"I wish I'd bought duct tape," he mutters. Then he licks the inside of my thigh and I think I'm a dripping amount of wet. I buck my hips towards him because really, it's about the only movement I can make. It's the only control I have on getting more. More friction, more of his mouth. More of his wicked perfect tongue.

"I don't want to play a board game tonight, Payton."

"No?"

"No, I think everything I want to play with is right here." He runs a hand down my leg, from hip to toe.

When he gets to my foot he massages his thumb into my arch. Firm, deep circular strokes followed by a press of his lips before he bends my knee and places my foot back on the bed.

Then he flicks my clit with his finger a moment before pinching my nipple. First one, then the other.

"Please," I beg. Please don't stop. Please do that again. Please fuck me until I can't remember my own name.

When he slides his finger inside of me I say thank you. Thank you, thank you, thank you. I'm so close, and then his finger is gone but his lips are back. Sucking and nipping and kissing. When his finger, wet with my own fluids, rims my asshole, I flinch. Of course I flinch. But I don't want him to stop, not in the least. My entire body is humming in sensation and anticipation. When he whispers, "Relax," I do. Then he works me up to the brink again, but this time I shatter with his finger in my ass and my clit between his teeth. He slips off the blindfold before he kisses me. He tastes like sex and forever.

Then he flips me over, slipping my hands free from the nylon restraint and rubbing my forearms before instructing me to get on all fours. He snags a condom and I want to tell him he doesn't need to, that I'm on the pill and I'm safe and we're married, but something holds me back. Because if he's not interested in coming inside of me it's really going to ruin the moment and I'm not in the headspace for that.

When he kneels behind me, hands wrapped around my waist, and thrusts deep, I'm not in any headspace at all. He uses my waist to rock me onto him at his desired speed, which is fast. Fast and hard, his fingers digging into my hips as he slams me onto his cock while he thrusts forward with his hips. The sound of our skin slapping echoes in the room, along with me. It's a lot of me moaning and sighing and begging. I'm not sure what I'm even begging for until he uses my hair to yank me upright and God, does that tug against my scalp nearly make me come again. He continues to drill me from behind, one hand wrapped in my hair as his other snakes around to work my clit. I'm so embarrassingly wet. Messy wet as he slides two fingers between my lips and tweaks my clit until I'm clenching so hard around him I feel like I might break. He pumps into me twice more before I feel him shudder, until the hand in my hair loosens, until I'm facedown on the bed, Vince on top of me, still inside of me, but done.

"Well, fuck." He brushes my hair out of the way and kisses the back of my neck. I shiver and wonder if I can die from orgasming.

Vince cleans us up. He gets up to dispose of the condom and comes back with a warm washcloth which he uses to clean me. "I can get up," I protest. Because no one has ever done that for me before and if he doesn't love me back I might die. I love him. I fucking love him and I don't even care how stupid and unpredictable love is. How uncertain and fragile and without guarantee.

"Sure you can," Vince agrees, which is kind because we both know it's a lie, "but I'm already here." He winks when he says it, accompanied by a wicked little grin. God, he just made a joke while cleaning me up after sex so I don't have to move. If I didn't already love him that alone would be enough to do it.

When he's done he gets back into my bed and I snuggle into his side and it's all so fucking normal and perfect. He laces his fingers with mine on his chest and we talk. He uses his other hand to play with my hair and I'm not sure if I want to fall asleep or stay awake forever so this night never ends.

When he tells me he'll be traveling next week I know I have to say something. Now, before he leaves, because he'll be gone an entire week clear across the state on some trial he's consulting on. Maybe it's too soon, but fuck it. Maybe my decision-making skills are shit but my spontaneity skills have served me well.

"You know how when you meet someone new, you're on your best behavior? How things are a little awkward because you're still feeling the other person out?"

"This has been you on your best behavior?" He can't hide the alarm on his face and I slap his chest with my open palm.

"No! That's my point. I've never felt that way with you. From the very first day I felt like myself."

Vince slow-blinks at me, his features relaxing.

"I think I'm falling in love with you."

"Do you?" Vince rolls us over so he's on top, brushing my hair back from my face. Then he kisses me, his lips brushing softly against mine. It makes me crazy, the soft caress of his lips in direct contrast of the hardness of his body, pressed against mine. The way his cock rests against my stomach, getting harder by the second.

"I do. I am." I'm distracted by his kisses and his cock, but I want him to know how I feel. "Which is good because I think fate wanted us to be together."

"Fate?" Vince pauses in kissing me, another frown marring his brow.

"Hmhmm." I trace the line on his forehead with

my fingertip. He nods, but in a distracted way, so I'm not sure we're on the same page about the contribution of destiny. But it's fine because destiny doesn't really care what you think about it, it just does its thing without your approval anyway.

Besides which, he's rolling another condom on so we can talk about destiny later.

By later I mean much, much later because his stamina on round two is off the charts. Life could not be going better for me. I'm capable of multiple orgasms and I'm in love with my husband. A man who makes me believe forevers might just exist.

Until destiny delivers a turd directly to my doorstep. A turd in the form of annulment papers.

TWENTY-SIX

VINCE LEFT ON Monday.

That part was fine. The trial, he'd mentioned the trial. He'd mentioned Reno. He'd mentioned he'd miss me. Isn't that what he'd said? *I'll miss you, gorgeous.* I'd grinned like a silly swan when he'd said it. Secure in where we were headed. Secure that his feelings for me were at the very least on the same game board as my feelings for him. But maybe I'd overwhelmed him with my silly proclamation of love. With my overactive imagination and demands for his time. With me.

Why? Why had I been sure?

I'll miss you.

Miss you forever?

He'd never mentioned that I'd be served with paperwork. Paperwork that would end our marriage. No, not just end it. Undo it.

Is it better to have loved and lost or to have never loved at all?

Lost is the answer here, because at least that's real. At least that happened. An annulment is nothing; it's a footnote on a Wikipedia page. It's official legal paperwork declaring that something was so insignificant as to have not existed. That it never should have happened to begin with. Maybe we were on different game boards after all. Maybe I was playing the game of Life and he was playing Operation because I feel like I'm a moment away from being shocked as Vince removes my heart.

He argues with people for a living and he couldn't talk to me himself?

That's so... insulting.

Is it because I distracted him with sex all week? He had to wait until he was six hours away and then have me served? Do you know how that feels? You probably don't. I hope you don't because it feels terrible. Awful. The worst ever.

"Are you Payton Tanner?" That's what I was greeted with when I opened my door this morning. I was less than a minute from leaving for work when my bell rang. I thought the guy worked for the apartment complex—that was my first thought when he spoke because how else would a stranger at my door know my name?

"You've been served," he said, thrusting a manila envelope into my hands and walking away. A very familiar manila envelope, because it looked exactly like the one Vince dropped on my countertop a week and a half earlier.

Those words are terrifying, by the way. *You've been served*. I know they're just words, but until they happen to you you have no idea how you'll react. How your heart will pound in overdrive the second your brain realizes that something serious is taking place.

They're just words.

I think I'm falling in love with you. Those are just words too. Unrequited words.

We'd talked or texted every night he'd been gone. Every freaking night. When he'd called on Monday night I'd smiled throughout the call because I'd loved hearing his voice over the phone. Loved knowing he'd wanted to talk to me when he couldn't see me. Loved knowing that he'd made time for me even though he had an insanely busy week in Reno.

Tuesday night we'd exchanged a series of racy texts. Racy, dirty, lusty texts.

Or maybe, maybe that was my imagination? Maybe *I wish you were here so I could bend you over and give you my cock* really meant *I'm horny*, not *I wish you were here*.

Or maybe he was telling me that he did want me, but not in the way I want him. There's so much to Vince I still don't know. Maybe I don't know anything.

I text him, in case you're thinking you'd react differently. That you'd pick up the phone and call. Or wait until he's back in town and ask him about it face to face. Or maybe you think you'd jump on a plane and fly to Reno, searching every courtroom until you found him.

I'm a reasonable person. So I texted.

Me: got the paperwork

And then I waited. I waited twenty minutes before sending a second text. I drove to work, alone with my overactive imagination. Shaky with nerves. Wondering if I was imagining this entire thing. If I was imagining how good things were between me and Vince. If I was imagining the paperwork that was sticking out of my handbag, even now. Mocking me as I side-eyed it while coasting through the parking garage at work, looking for a good space.

Except it's still there when I park. *District Court.*

Clark County, Nevada. Vincent Thomas Rossi vs Payton Elizabeth Tanner.

It's sweet the way he knows my middle name. I didn't know his. Why did I never ask? I had an entire ten days up to this point to ask. I'm a terrible wife.

I put the car into park and check my phone. No reply. It's fine. It's so fine. I get it. I want him to know I get it so I send another text.

Me: it's fine

I toss my phone into my bag and head inside. I don't have time to dawdle while I hope for a reply because I've got less than ten minutes to get to my desk. Getting served with annulment paperwork has thrown me a bit behind schedule this morning. I set my phone face down onto my desk and deposit my handbag into the bottom drawer. I wiggle the mouse so my computer will spring to life. I brood, because it's not fine. I watch the clock on my computer and flip my phone over checking for a text no fewer than five times. Nothing. Every minute is an eternity in which I envision ways this ends badly.

An hour later when Vince calls, I nearly send him to voicemail. Mostly because my imagination is raging out of control. But as I've said, I'm very reasonable. Or at least on the scale of reasonableness. The low end, I know. I'm not a reasonableness overachiever but I have a very firm grasp on the concept.

So I answer the phone.

"Hey," I say. Because that's how you answer the phone when your husband who you've just met but have fallen very hard for has you served with annulment paperwork. Annulment is a word that means to take something back. To cancel. To retract. To reverse. To undo.

It's the worst word ever.

It's the worst feeling ever.

Worse than the time the Girl Troopers dumped me. Worse than every time my parents got divorced. Worse than being cheated on sophomore year in college. Worse is a word that means icky. The ickiest.

"Payton." He exhales into the phone. He has a great phone voice. Deep and seductive. Composed and captivating. But right now he sounds rushed, distracted. "What paperwork, Payton?" There's a lot of background noise. Voices, commotion, possibly the ding of an elevator. He's busy, clearly he's busy. So busy he forgot today was the day I was being served. Or perhaps he didn't know when I'd get the paperwork. If I'd gone to work even ten minutes earlier, I'd have missed the server this morning.

I allow myself a brief fantasy in which I did leave for work early. A fantasy in which the server spent weeks attempting to find me, never in the right place at the right time. Weeks in which Vince fell madly in love with me and put a halt to the unraveling of our marriage. 'Madly' is the only word in that sentence that makes any sense at all though. A drunken lustful night cannot possibly work out in a rosy happily-ever-after way.

"The annulment paperwork. I've got it."

"What do you mean you've got it?" I hear him tell someone in the background that he needs a minute, the words not spoken directly into the receiver, but as if he's tilted the phone away from his lips. I can picture him, even without seeing him. I can picture what he's wearing and how he's standing. I can imagine his shoes, polished, and his tie, knotted. I wonder if he's wearing a tie I've seen before, or one I haven't. Likely one I haven't because he surely owns more ties than I've had time to see. I imagine his phone pressed to his ear, held in place by two long fingers and a bent thumb. No case on the phone. A thousand-dollar piece of glass and metal that he carries without a case. I asked him once if he worried about breaking it. He shrugged like it was nothing and said he'd get a new one if something happened to it. I didn't think he'd break it, though. I thought the phone simply knew better than to dare slip from his grasp.

"The annulment paperwork. I was served this morning, on my way to work."

"Fuck." This is muttered straight into the receiver, but I get the impression he's saying it to himself as opposed to me. "Payton, about that." He sounds harassed, and I hate it. Vince never sounds hurried. He never sounds like he's anything less than one hundred percent in control and I hate that I'm his speed bump, an interruption to his day. To his life. I've put him in this position, saddled with a pretend wife he didn't ask for. I'm a husband predator. Targeting unsuspecting men for drunken shenanigans that end in vows of forever. That's what I did, right? I saw him in the lobby at work, fell instantly in lust with him and then decided fate, my libido, and my love for instant marriage reality shows meant we had a shot at being together forever.

Thinking I could circumvent failure with random luck and lust. Thinking statistically we had as good a chance as anyone. Thinking I could use alcohol as my scapegoat.

Stupid.

I'm embarrassed. So embarrassed that he doesn't feel the way I feel, because that's what it boils down to, doesn't it? Saturday night I told him I was falling in love with him and not only did he not say it back, he questioned my pledge of love. What did he say? *Are you? Do you?* It didn't bother me in the moment. It didn't feel awkward when he simply smiled and fucked me into multiple orgasms as a response.

"It's fine," I interrupt him before he has a chance for a lengthy explanation. He's not breaking up with me. At least, I don't think he is. He can't possibly be, we just had phone sex twelve hours ago. I think he's just slowing us down. He's busy and I'm a handful on the best of days.

Today is not my best of days. But still, I dig deep into my small vat of reasonableness.

"What do you mean it's fine?" he asks and now his tone seems annoyed—with me. The word 'fine' is enunciated with more edge than I'm used to from Vince. Unless I'm imagining things. I do tend to run wild with my imagination and my reasonableness vat is closer to the size of a coffee cup at this moment. Could last night have been goodbye phone sex? God, that cannot be a thing can it? No one does that.

Then I hear him speaking to someone he's with, the phone pulled just far enough away that it increases the background noise and lowers the volume of Vince's voice, but I can still hear every word. "Are you still on the phone with Gwen? Have her hold. I need to talk to her when I'm done with this call," is what he says.

Gwen? It takes me zero point zero two seconds to locate that name in my brain. Gwen is the name of his ex. How many women living in the Las Vegas area could possibly be named Gwen? It's not that common. Or popular, Gwen. I hate you and your dumb name because my math-ing tells me that it's likely this Gwen and his ex Gwen are the same person. This all just became so much ickier because why does he need to talk to Gwen about anything? Why does he even talk to Gwen at all?

"What did you mean by it's fine, Payton?" Vince prompts because I've still not replied, having been thrown by his tone and my wayward thoughts.

"I meant that it's fine, Vince. I meant that I get it. We did a drunk crazy thing, I know it's not forever. We're having a good time though, right?"

"A good time," he repeats into the receiver and I can't tell by his voice if it's a statement, a question or an accusation.

"A great time?" I offer because I'm feeling him out, because I'm feeling confused by the events of the last couple of hours, by his tone, by everything. Because I'm at work and I'm trying to keep my voice low and this is all so weird. This vibe right now is throwing me for a loop because I'm not used to it. Things between us were so normal. Minus the impromptu wedding, me running out the next morning, the annulment paperwork that he brought over, then took back and never brought up again. Besides all that, super normal. So I'm not sure how to deal with this, with him, in this moment. "It's okay, is all I meant. It's fine. I understand."

"What the hell is it that you think you understand, Payton?"

God. I don't know! I don't know what I think I understand anymore. And perfect timing, now my boss is standing next to my cube looking from the cell phone in my hand to her watch and back again. She points a thumb in the direction of the conference room. Right, I forgot we have a team meeting in... one minute.

"Don't worry about it," I tell Vince. "We can talk about it when you get back."

There's a silence so long I'd wonder if he hung up except I can still hear the background noise on his end. He snaps, "Tell her to hold," at someone in his vicinity.

"You are a whirlwind of chaos, Payton. You're a goddamn tornado of pandemonium and disarray and I—" He cuts himself off with a harsh inhale. Then he blows it out on a long exhale and I imagine he's rubbing two fingers across his forehead and shaking his head at my obnoxiousness. "We'll talk when I get back. I've got to go."

I know you do, Vince. Gwen is holding, after all. Gwen is Holding would make a great band name. A punky angsty band, specializing in teenage breakup songs.

"Try not to do anything impetuous or reckless today, if you can manage it," he says by way of goodbye.

"Like marry a stranger?" I respond a bit sulkily because I am sulky. I'm on guard and confused and feeling every word that means the opposite of reasonable.

"Like that, yes," he answers after a long pause. Then he hangs up.

Okay then. I sigh as I push my chair back and stand, gathering my things for the department meeting. At the last minute I grab the annulment papers from my purse and slide them into the stack of papers I'm bringing to the meeting. These things are boring as hell, I might as well use the time to scan over the paperwork. Familiarize myself. Maybe calm down a little and decipher whether that entire crazy exchange really happened. Whether I overreacted and blew it out of proportion or whether I haven't reacted enough. Like Gwen—what does she have to do with this? Probably nothing, right? But why does he speak to her? That's annoying. Maybe old people talk to their exes but I don't care for it. I cross my arms and huff while I try to look like I'm interested in this meeting.

There's probably something really wrong with him anyway. He's far too perfect to have just been hanging around, single, waiting for me to show up for thirty-seven years. Right? I'm a disaster and he's perfect. And Jesus Christ, the things he does to me with his tongue. And those fingers. And his—well, I can't even think about his penis right now because I'm at work and I have enough problems without spontaneously combusting into orgasm in the middle of this meeting. The point is, he's probably super annoying in all sorts of ways I just haven't figured out yet.

Probably.

So fucking annoying the way he brings groceries over. And cooks. And cleans up. And plays board games with me. And engages me in meaningful conversations before taking me to bed and doing all manner of filthy things to me until I come—always before he does. Yup. He's a jerk. Women probably dump him all the time.

I heave an exasperated sigh until Mark elbows me, reminding me I'm in a meeting. I wiggle my pen around on my notepad, pretending to listen. I'm not a terrible employee, it's just that we're covering the same material that was sent via email two days ago. Maybe some people need to have the email read aloud to them. I do not. I'm an excellent reader, it's one of my strengths.

Which makes me think. I should look at this paperwork a bit closer, shouldn't I? I bet he filed it that very first day. I mean, I know he did, don't I? He tossed it on my kitchen counter and said we needed to talk about it. Except that we didn't talk about it and then he took it with him and we never even discussed what the 'it' was.

But it doesn't take a genius to figure it out. Of course he'd have filed annulment paperwork. He's a freaking lawyer, he probably filed it himself that Sunday afternoon after I ran out of my apartment without my bra on. He probably went home, fired up his laptop and completed the paperwork, and why wouldn't he? I was a crazy girl who tricked him into a drunken marriage and then ran off once I slept with him.

Honestly, I'm not sure why he's put up with me this long. I'm good in bed, but I'm not *that* good. I don't know any tricks or anything. I can't deepthroat, like not even a little. Don't get me wrong, no one's ever complained, and I think I've perfected a nice hand-mouth combination that might give the illusion that I'm taking on more than I am. But there's no 'fuck my mouth, sir' offers happening, I can promise you that.

I'm a terrible cook and I already admitted I have no interest in picking up his dry cleaning. I'd have kept that fact to myself if I'd realized he wore nothing but suits and freaking pressed shirts on the daily. Not that I've changed my mind about picking up dry cleaning, but I'd have at least kept up the illusion that I *might* pick up his dry cleaning for a little longer.

But still, he seems to like me. Maybe he doesn't love me, but who could blame him? We haven't even hit our two-week anniversary yet. I slide the papers out of the envelope and read them, line for line. It's really boring and filled with the words 'defendant' and 'plaintiff' over and over again. I know it's just legal jargon but it's sad.

When I look a little closer I notice something else. Rossi Law Firm on South 4th Street is listed on the paperwork. But it also lists Gwen Jones, Esq. And a Nevada bar number for Gwen Jones. And here on the final page it states Gwen Jones, Esq, attorney for the plaintiff Vincent Thomas Rossi.

I'm positive I'm red with humiliation or possibly rage. *Tell Gwen to hold, I need to talk to her.*

That fucking fucker. He had his ex prepare the paperwork? I wasn't even worth seven hundred dollars of his time to complete the paperwork himself? He had his ex do it for him? His ex who works for him? At his law firm?

Did they laugh about it? About me? Did he stroll into her office that Monday morning and regale her with stories of his weekend of regret? About the silly girl who couldn't stop throwing herself at him all weekend? Did they talk about lawyerly things as he told her he'd accidentally married a girl who plans weddings for a living due to a whirlwind of booze and lust?

Kismet is dead. Not even a bathtub full of Cheez-Its could make this better.

TWENTY-SEVEN

"DID YOU GET everything you needed or did you want me to grab a slice of pizza for you?"

I scowl at Mark, because that was not a genuine offer. It was an offer laced with sarcasm and judgment over my lunch choices. I've got a bowl of pasta and an entire turkey dinner with mashed potatoes and gravy, green beans and stuffing. And a cupcake. Fine, it's two cupcakes but I'm in crisis and I fit it all on one tray so I don't know what he's nagging me about. One tray equals one lunch, everyone knows that. I shoot him a nasty glare as I pick up my tray and navigate the employee cafeteria, looking for a good seat. We're having a late lunch because our department meeting droned on forever, unlike my marriage, which only droned on for twelve days.

On the bright side, I'm already on the fourth stage of grief which is depression and carbohydrates. I think I might be a grieving overachiever, which is sorta sad, but I'm going to add it to my list of strengths anyway because I should still get credit for it.

Which reminds me of something else I should do.

"We should look Gwen up on the internet," I announce once I've located a suitable table for eating and griping. That table is a booth along the far wall of the employee dining room because booths are ideal for private bitching sessions. And unbuttoning your pants for optimal caloric intake.

Lydia ate lunch an hour ago, which is a blessing because I cannot fake being happy right now and I still haven't told her I'm married. Which is just as well, because I'm almost unmarried so why even bring it up at all?

Acceptance. It's the fifth stage of grief. I'm going to pretend I haven't hit it, because I'm not skipping the carbohydrate stage. Fuck that.

"Sure." Mark slides into the booth across from me. "That sounds right."

"Are you any good at math?" I ask while I open the internet browser on my phone. "How many boxes of Cheez-Its do you think I'd need to fill a bathtub, with me inside the tub?"

"I'm not answering that."

"I was thinking twenty boxes, but then I wondered if that would be enough to be satisfying or if it would only barely cover the bottom of the tub. What do you think?"

Mark sighs as he twists the cap off of a bottle of water, as if he's resigning himself to having a conversation about the volume of crackers required to fill a bathtub. "I think it'd take a hundred boxes or more."

"God, that's like three hundred dollars in crackers. Do you think I can claim that expense on my annulment?"

"I don't think you can claim anything on an annulment. For starters you're referring to an annulment like it's a tax return, which it's not. If you're asking if you can request that Vince pay for a hundred boxes of Cheez-Its as some kind of financial settlement for your marriage, the answer is no. That's not how an annulment works."

"This day just keeps getting worse and worse," I groan as I type 'Rossi Law Firm' into my internet search. It's a really nice website and a really large law firm based on the number of attorneys on staff. If I was a supportive wife and not a bitter soon-to-be ex-wife I'd be really impressed. I click on the tab labeled 'attorneys' and there she is, Gwen Jones. There's a picture of her. She's blonde, went to law school at UCLA and I hate her. Those are the first things I notice. She's a partner, which is super annoying and earns her another point in the 'I hate her' column. She specializes in family law and in her free time she sits on the board of directors for Girl Troopers of southern Las Vegas.

Who the hell can compete with that?

Not me. The full extent of my volunteer efforts is returning shopping carts to the shopping cart corral after I've put my groceries in the car and really, I don't think that counts.

"See, this is the kind of woman he should be with." I hold the phone up for Mark to scan. "Not a party-planning crazy girl like myself. A lawyer should have a serious wife."

"Okay, simmer down. Don't go all Elle Woods in *Legally Blonde* on me. You are jumping to some really wild conclusions here, even for you."

"Maybe." I twirl a bite of spaghetti around my fork and stuff it in my mouth. Then I type 'Gwen Jones, ESQ' into my Google search and click on images. And there it is, a picture of Vince and Gwen together. It was taken at a red-carpet charity event. There's a super cute backdrop for the photo and I wonder who planned that event because I would love to know who did their graphics. I pass the phone over to Mark again. "I was right about them being together though. There they are." I slump in the booth and drag my fork through the mashed potatoes.

"Three years ago," Mark says, looking at the photo. "That event was three years ago." He rolls his eyes in my face as he sets the phone down on the table.

"I don't care how long ago it was, he shouldn't have had his ex-girlfriend file the paperwork for the annulment. It's... rude." I finally decide on 'rude' as the best way to sum up 'inconsiderate,' 'boorish,' 'ignorant' and 'insulting.' Then I make a face at Mark, daring him to disagree.

"This is not the work wife I didn't ask to fake-marry." Mark shakes his head with a sad look of disappointment on his face.

"See!" I throw my hands in the air as if this proves everything. "I am a husband predator! I prey on innocent men and trick them into marriage!"

"No, I meant since when do you just sit back and passively let anything happen? You didn't do it with me. You told me we were friends on your second day of work. After I made that joke about raccoons, you simply said, 'Mark, we're friends now.'"

"Oh, yeah." I grin. "Raccoons are really funny though. Plus they've got those silly little masks that make it look like they're gonna rob a bank." I motion in the air as if I've got tiny raccoon paws.

Mark stares at me, nonplussed.

"Did you know that raccoon moms raise their children on their own?" I nod solemnly while Mark continues to stare at me while he chews. "People should be more understanding when a raccoon is digging through the trash or trying to get a slice of pizza. Single mom-ing isn't easy."

"The point is," Mark continues, "you didn't ask me to be your friend, you told me. Which is really obnoxious now that I think about it, but it's part of your charm. And then you did it again when you made me your work husband."

I nod. I am both obnoxious and charming. And possibly near the high end of the aggressive scale.

"When the Harrison-Nichols wedding was nearly called off over a dispute about where to seat the groom's fraternity brothers, you didn't just give in. You created a new seating chart and managed to set up the bride's cousin with one of those frat boys."

That's true. I did do that. They were super compatible on paper. By on paper I mean I reviewed the Instagram accounts of each guest not bringing a date and then paired them up on the seating chart based on my objective opinion about who was most likely to couple up. It's only been three weeks, but according to my stalking via Instagram things are looking really good for the bride's cousin and the fraternity brother I paired her up with.

"When the Bronsons requested—one day before their vow renewal—that it snow inside a Las Vegas ballroom, did you tell them no? No, you did not, Payton Tanner. You found a snow machine in Las Vegas on a Friday afternoon and had it set up in the ballroom before you left work that night. Because you are not a quitter."

That's true too.

"And when fate placed you in Vince's office, you married him. Just like you said you would."

"Okay, whoa." I hold up a hand in the universal

'hold the heck on' gesture. "I was mostly kidding about that. I mean sure, I was open to marrying him the first time I saw him because of the kismet, you know? And because of the sexual attraction. But I meant if it worked out, like if we met and dated and I didn't drive him crazy and he didn't annoy me and if the sex was half as good as I envisioned it being. I didn't mean I was going to trick him into marrying me on our first date."

"Exactly."

"Exactly what? What point did you just prove?"

"That you're not a husband predator and you're not a quitter."

That's true, I suppose. I didn't set out to trick him into marrying me. It's not my fault that he didn't pick option A and let me get a tiger tattooed onto my ass. No one forced him into becoming the tattoo police.

"Maybe not, but how do I know if kismet is just fucking with me?"

"Pffft. As if kismet would dare. As if fate stands a chance against Payton on a mission."

Hmm, that's valid.

"I'm so confused, Mark. Loving Vince is a lot like shopping at Target."

"Sure." Mark nods, his face devoid of judgment because he's an excellent work spouse. "How so exactly?"

"Well, I had no idea I needed him until I saw him. You know? I was just merrily living my life without Vince and I thought I was happy. I thought I had everything I needed. But then poof, there he was and I was like, I *need* this guy. I cannot live without *this* guy. So I put him in my cart and married him and now I will absolutely die if he drops me off at the return desk and I have to spend the rest of my life walking around the store trying to find a better Vince than the Vince I already had."

Mark simply blinks at me from across the table and I think it's because that analogy was so profound he can't find the words to reply, but it's fine, because I have a plan.

TWENTY-EIGHT

"I NEED YOU TO find someone for me," I announce as I sail into Canon's office and help myself to one of the guest chairs facing his desk.

"Vince is in Reno consulting on a case."

"I know where Vince is," I reply, not bothering to hide my exasperation. "I need to know where Carol is."

"Who the hell is Carol?" Canon stops typing and looks up from his monitor. He leans back in his chair and steeples his fingers together and I have the distinct impression I've caught his interest. Mostly because he's a nosey motherfucker.

"My life coach."

"Your life coach." Canon nods slowly and raises an eyebrow and I get the impression I've just made his day. "Do go on."

"Yes. My life coach. I need to find her ASAP because I need life advice."

"Have you tried calling her?"

"I lost her number." I toss my hands up in the air as if it could happen to anyone.

"How did you lose a number you've dialed from your phone? It stays in there forever. Outgoing calls. You want me to hack your phone again and look it up for you?" He leans back over his keyboard as if he's going to do just that.

"No! Don't do that!" I wave my hand in a stop gesture. God, Canon is a pain in the ass. A pain in the ass with fantastic stalking skills, I remind myself. "I never schedule appointments by phone, so I don't have her number."

"Sure. You schedule via email then?"

"Okay." I heave a sigh because I can't really see any way around this. "The thing is..." I begin but Canon interrupts.

"I cannot wait to hear the thing." He's smiling and I know he's going to enjoy this far too much, but I'm desperate, so I level a look at him implying he should shut up if he wants to hear the thing. He grins like an asshole and leans back in his chair.

"The thing is, Carol wasn't exactly my life coach."

"Elaborate."

"I was just sorta life coach-sampling." I pick at a non-existent piece of lint on my knee and avoid looking at Canon. When I can't take the silence anymore I risk a glance in his direction.

"Tell me everything. I need a full visual picture."

"Uggh, you're so annoying."

"Spill or I don't help."

I begrudgingly explain the entirety of fate providing me with a couple of sample life coaching sessions while Canon interrupts to ask questions. When I'm done and when he's finished laughing, he tells me I have potential in surveillance if I ever want to make a career change to the security field. Which is nice. I'm adding surveillance skills to my list of strengths because really, it's not a bad skill to have and it's good to know I have diversification abilities.

"So you want to find Carol because you're in search of life advice you can't gain from eavesdropping?"

"Sampling. I was sampling."

"Right. Sampling."

"But I'm ready to upgrade to a real appointment because I need her to help me identify my strengths. Like a comprehensive list, not just an overview."

"Why is that exactly?"

"So I can present it to Vince."

"Sure. Is this some kind of fetish thing? Some kind of kinky roleplaying involving paperwork and spanking? Actually, don't answer that. It's more information than I want to know."

"Can you find Carol or not?"

"You want me to find a life coach named Carol, no last name, no phone number, email or office address?"

"I was hoping you could."

"Of course I can, Jesus." Canon rolls his eyes and taps at his keyboard while muttering about people misusing his skill set. "Tell me what kinds of things were talked about during the sessions."

"The usual. Career goals, decision-making skills, the usual."

"I have hits on two life coaches in Las Vegas named Carol." Canon tilts his monitor so I can see the images he's pulled up. Neither are my life coach. After a series of false tries, finally Canon turns the monitor and it's her. It's Carol!

"That's her!" I bounce in my seat in excitement. "Can you find a phone number or email?"

"Carol is not a life coach, Payton," Canon responds as he turns the monitor back.

"Yes, she is! She's really good!"

"What other kinds of things were talked about at these supposed life coaching sessions?"

"I don't know, I didn't catch everything. Sampling is more of an overview appointment."

"Stuff like sales goals? Performance rewards? Commissions?"

"Maybe? I kinda tuned that stuff out because I was mainly interested in the personal growth. I think Meghan was saving to buy a timeshare though. I don't know."

"Carol sells essential oils, Payton. She's not a life coach. She's an essential oil team leader. Meghan is one of her commissioned sales reps."

What?

Canon flips the screen around again and there's Carol. Apparently I can get an appointment with her if I'm willing to buy a hundred-and-sixty-dollar starter kit.

"Carol isn't a life coach?"

"No."

"I almost joined a cult?"

"I think 'cult' might be a real big leap. You might have been headed towards obtaining a diffuser and a second job, but I think that's the extent of it."

"Huh." I slump in the chair because I can't believe how crazy I am. "I'm such an idiot."

"I think you're actually quite clever."

I groan and drop my head back to stare at the ceiling in Canon's office. This is fine, I don't need Carol. I was just having a crisis of confidence, which is ridiculous because I've totally got this.

"You're Vince's best friend, right?"

"We haven't made it Facebook official yet"—Canon shrugs—"but it's looking good."

"The thing is, Canon, is that I legiterally love him."

"As one does, loveable bastard that Vince is. Oh,

that reminds me, I've got something for you." He slides open a desk drawer and pulls something out, smiling as he glances at it before he sliding it across the desktop to me. It's an employee ID. My employee ID, but with my new last name, Rossi. Payton Rossi.

"I don't need this." I sigh as I'm hit with a wave of emotions. This is the first time I've seen my married name on anything. Minus the eighty-seven times that I practice-wrote it during meetings this week, but that wasn't printed on something official like an employment ID card. I exhale into a big slump in the chair. "Vince is dumping me."

"I doubt that's true." Canon seems really unmoved about my impending break-up. I'd have thought he'd care more since he was the maid of honor at our wedding, but no. He's swiveling in his chair, acting as if we're discussing the cafeteria meatloaf.

"It's true! Well, partially true. I think he likes me." I pause as I say that because it needs a rephrase. "I know he likes me. He's done nothing but show me how much he likes me, until today. Today has been iffy but he sounded stressed and maybe he's not a phone person. Is he? Do you guys talk on the phone?"

"Every night at ten. We discuss the day and how it made us feel before planning our outfits for the next day."

"He's kinda moody on the phone," I continue, ignoring Canon. "I think the husband thing might be too much for him. I'm hoping to convince him to boyfriend me, I just need a second chance."

"How much do you know about Vince?"

"God, don't nag me, Canon. I've known him for less than two weeks. I'll admit we're on the lower end of the getting-to-know you scale, but sometimes you just know. I mean other people, not you. You're still single so obviously you haven't you haven't experienced what just knowing feels like."

"Sometimes I meet a woman I just know I'm meant to have sex with once, then never see again. Does that count?"

"Sorta?" I scrunch my nose up while I think about it. "I'm not the just knowing police, but it sounds like you at least understand the concept. Don't worry though, I didn't believe in forever until I met Vince so there's still hope for you. I used to believe that love only lasted for spans of one to ten years, but Vince changed that for me. He made me believe that shooting for forever is worth the risk."

Canon stares at me from across the desk, his expression thoughtful.

"Let me tell you a few things about Vince Rossi."

TWENTY-NINE

IN THE END I decide that a hundred boxes of Cheez-Its is extreme. That's a lie. I would have gotten a hundred boxes but there were only sixty-seven boxes of Cheez-Its on the store shelf and I decided sixty-seven wasn't enough to fill the tub and it would be rude to wipe out the entire stock of Cheez-Its when some other girl may be having a crisis and need one of those boxes. So in order not to contribute to a cheese-flavored cracker shortage, I limited my purchase to three.

They're lined up now on the edge of my tub. One box each of original cheese, extra-toasty cheese and white cheddar cheese. As for me, I'm in the tub, fully dressed. The tub is devoid of water but it's still quite comforting, like a hug. The pillow helps, as does the blanket. The couch would admittedly have been more comfortable but it doesn't have the same self-soothing appeal as the tub. The tub is like a nest where I can hole up while I reflect on my life choices.

I know it's weird, but filling the entire tub with crackers would have been weirder, so I'm calling this a win because I really need a win. Fuck Carol and her essential oils.

It turns out that Vince is a bit of a do-gooder. It turns out that strippers aren't his hobby, helping people is his hobby. I thought he was a bit of a bad boy—a strip-club-owning lawyer. A sexy rogue.

But he's not. He's perfect is what he is. My do-gooder husband. I know, I know. How much do-gooding could a strip club owner-slash-lawyer do?

A lot.

He's on the board of directors at three local charities.

His law firm has done more pro bono work than any other law firm in Nevada for four years running.

He funnels every dollar of profit from the club into scholarships for the employees. All of them: the dancers, the bartenders, the servers. Anyone who wants an education gets one. In fact, every employee is hired with the understanding that they will take advantage of it and move on. That it's a stepping stone, not a career.

So yeah, I guess attempting to learn how to pole-dance wasn't that impressive, and was possibly offensive.

And we already know that the sum total of my volunteering is returning the grocery cart to the cart corral.

My husband is so far out of my league.

The real problem? He didn't tell me any of this himself, I heard it all from Canon.

Why wouldn't he tell me all those good things about himself? Why wouldn't he share that? That's what stings. We talked all week. Talked and ate and talked and played games and talked and fucked.

But how much did he really share? How much did he open up? I thought it was a lot. We talked about his mom and growing up in Vegas and so many things. We talked about where he went to school and his hobbies. We specifically talked about the strip club and he never corrected me when I called it a hobby.

He sent me annulment paperwork without talking to me about it.

He didn't say he loved me back.

But then I remind myself of the way he acted, the way he made me feel. His actions tell me that he cares about me. That he's interested in me, that he likes me. He spent every single day with me until his business trip—and that wasn't just sex. It was so far from just sex. Maybe he's not ready to admit that he loves me yet, but he's well on his way. I'm sure of it. Mostly sure. Sure enough?

I never once saw where he lived. I asked him when I was going to see his place and he said it was a shithole. I asked him what he did with his seven-hundred-dollar-an-hour income if he lived in a shithole and he laughed. Said he had a condo downtown near his office. An expensive condo that was lifeless and cold compared to my apartment, but that I was welcome to see it anytime.

But then he sent me annulment paperwork, so maybe he didn't mean anytime. Maybe he meant he didn't want me to know where he lived.

They say that love conquers all, but that's a lie. Love fucks up all the time. I've seen firsthand how much love cannot conquer.

Love is an asshole.

THIRTY

ON SATURDAY I decide enough is enough. Winners never quit and quitters never win. Fine, I don't decide that at all, but I have to go to work. Because today is the hotel's grand opening gala and since I work in event planning, it's imperative that I'm there. Everyone in my department has a shift they need to cover today. I'm in charge of overseeing valet services from four till eight this evening.

I know, lame.

I don't even know anything about valet services, not really. But one member of the event planning staff will be stationed throughout the hotel for the entire day. Just on standby, really. I don't have to do anything but be on hand in case there's a car parking emergency.

Like I said, lame.

Someday I'll get the good assignments, like being the point person for the pop star who was hired to perform tonight. Until then, I'll rock the hell out of making sure everyone in valet services is hustling this afternoon and if an emergency arrives I'll be there to take care of it. By take care of it I mean I'll call my boss and relay what's happening. That's really the entirety of my assignment today.

Maybe I'll use the time to matchmake via

Instagram. I'm sure at least one of the valet guys could use my help, so the afternoon won't be a total waste. And afterwards I can attend the gala myself. Not that I'm really in the mood, not at all, but I'll go to see Lydia. She'll be there with Rhys and I'm sure he'll be busy and I'll get a few minutes to catch up with her and see how things are going between them.

So onwards and upwards and all that.

Vince texted and said he'd be home today. *I'll be home on Saturday*, the text read. I took it to mean he'd be flying home from Reno sometime on Saturday and would probably go to his place. Of course he'd go to his place, it's not as if he has things at my place. I'm sure we'll get together sometime this weekend and talk. God, I'm not in the mood for talking. The only talking I want to do is getting-to-know-you talking, not breaking-up-with-you talking. I'm not interested in that kind of talking, not at all.

But for today, work. Then the gala. Then I'll figure out what Vince and I are doing. I shower and do my hair, sweeping my hair up into a high bun. I spend extra time on my makeup and then select a fairly demure blush-colored dress that will work for both my afternoon responsibilities and as much of the gala that I want to stay at. It's got three-quarter sleeves and the skirt hits me mid-thigh. I slip my feet in a pair of nude heels and examine my reflection in the mirror.

I look very wife-y if I say so myself. It's a waste because Vince won't be seeing me tonight. Not unless he calls to apologize for having his ex-girlfriend submit our annulment paperwork, tells me he loves me and invites me over to sit on his face. I'm a bit of a dreamer so I primped and put on good underwear just in case.

On the way to work I swing through the Del Taco drive-thru to get an iced java and the first sip reminds me of Vince. It's stupid—I've had Del Taco with him once and without him forty or more times. Yet the second I take the first sip I remember that he brought me tacos. Tacos and my favorite iced coffee even though I drive him nuts when I rattle the ice around the cup.

When I get to work I park in the employee section of the garage and stop by my department to check in before I head down to valet. Honestly, I lucked out with this early coverage of the opening. The event isn't really kicking off until eight so I've got a while until things start hopping. I find the administrative offices closest to the valet area and introduce myself to the team lead, letting her know to holler if she needs anything. Then I find a place to observe while staying out of the way, sip my iced coffee and catch up on a few games of Words with Friends on my cell.

My game is interrupted by a text from Canon.

Canon: Nice dress. Very wifely.

I glance around, expecting to see him lounging against a wall somewhere, but I can't see him. That's when I realize he's watching me on a security camera.

Payton: Are you watching me on camera? Seriously, you need help.

Canon: ikr? I think I have a surveillance fetish.

Payton: you're fucking weird. Tell me where the camera is so I can flip you off.

Canon: Pfft. Where isn't the camera is more like it.

Payton: Weirdo.

Canon: I'm not the one who just played a two-letter word for five points. Have some pride.

Payton: you can see that?!?!?!

Canon: I can see everrrrrything from my surveillance kingdom.

Payton: ...

Canon: I've got a pop star and a former president due to arrive in the next hour. They were told to use the private entrance under the west parking garage, but if they miss the turn they may head for valet. Heads up.

Payton: thanks.

I spend the next few hours doing nothing because valet services really doesn't need any help. The parking garage for self-park and valet is nowhere near capacity and valet is on top of things, grabbing keys and handing out tickets within thirty seconds of each car that pulls in. It turns out that there is slightly more to my responsibilities than keeping an eye on any car parking emergencies. I'm also standing by in case a VIP guest needs something between their car and the lobby, where they're being greeted by a VIP liaison. As you'd expect, no one has needed anything during their twenty-foot walk to the door, so I'm mostly people-watching. The only celebrities arriving this early have been newspeople. I spotted an anchor from CNN and a reality TV star-turned-red carpet host for the E! Network, but otherwise, nada. Mark is overseeing valet from eight till midnight so I'm hovering near the valet desk people, watching and waiting on Mark to show up so I can hand over the reins.

Which is how I nearly run smack into Vince.

He's here. In a black suit and God help me he looks good. I catch him just as he slides out of his car and scans the area with a slow sweep of his eyes. I duck behind the valet desk before he can see me, and I don't even know why I'm hiding. I'm so surprised to see him that I'm thrown off guard and my heart is racing like I just ran half a mile in heels. My phone dings an incoming text.

Canon: Hey, FYI, your husband is on his way here.

Payton: Why are you such a dick at giving me a heads-up? He's already here, but you know that, don't you!?!?!?

Canon: Yeah, but it's more fun for me this way.

Payton: dick!

Canon: He's inside now if you want to stop

crouching behind the valet stand.

I hold my middle finger up over my head, then stand and exhale loudly. Okay, so Vince is here. That's good? That's good. I straighten my dress and contemplate what I want to say to Vince. I don't get very far in my contemplations when Mark arrives, so I bring him up to date on the whole lot of nothing that's been going on, then I head inside. I detour to my desk on the third floor to grab my handbag, but my boss is in a chatty mood so by the time I head down to the party it's nearly nine. And I'm jumpy.

The thing is, when you're sort of looking for someone and sort of avoiding them at the same time, it tends to make a person a little tense. Like when you go to a haunted house and you know none of it's real and you're not actually in danger of dying, but you still jump when a teenager dressed as a werewolf yells, "Boo!" Kinda like that.

We're expecting up to five thousand people tonight and there's at least half that many crowding the ballroom space, so when I walk into the room and see Vince it's perfectly normal to pretend I don't see him and dash in the other direction.

Perfectly normal.

I can feel your judge-y eyes, but unless you married a man the day you met him, yet somehow, some way, fell in actual real love with him even though love is terrifying and unpredictable and doesn't come with a guarantee, you don't know how you'd react the first time you saw him after he sent you annulment papers.

So I run. Not far, just to the other side of the ballroom. Then to the ballroom across the hall where they've got an opening act playing for the pop star.

And then back to the main ballroom, where I run smack into Lydia.

"Hey!" She grabs me into a quick hug and then asks who I'm avoiding.

"Vince."

"He's here?"

"He's freaking everywhere."

"I think he's friends with Canon," she says with a small frown, probably wondering why the guy who helped her set up her fake virginity auction to Rhys, but whom she still may think is an actual pimp, is here.

"Yeah, that's probably why he's here," I lie because I haven't brought Lydia up to speed on anything and now doesn't really seem like the time, does it? *Hey, Vince doesn't actually broker hookers, and by the way I married him.* Seems awkward, right? When a tray of d'oeuvres passes by I grab one and shove it into my mouth to buy some time.

"Are you in some sort of trouble?" Lydia asks, eyes narrowing on me in concern. Damn, I forgot that she can be really observant when she's not completely oblivious. It's sorta all-or-nothing with her.

"Of course not." I shake my head. "I'm taking care of it."

"Taking care of what?" She's definitely suspicious now. And nosey. Somebody named Lydia is getting a nosey badge on Monday, I can promise you that.

"The thing," I respond as I snag a glass of champagne off a passing tray. "I'm going to fix it. It's just turning out to be a bit more complicated than one would think." God, if that isn't the truth I don't know what is. Marriage is super complicated.

"What thing, Payton? What's going on?"

"Nothing. I'll tell you later," I insist. Then I spot Vince headed in my direction and he looks annoyed. Real annoyed. The thing is, I don't think we need to talk about our future when he's in a bad mood. That doesn't make sense, so maybe I'll just slip out of here, go home and I'll talk to Vince tomorrow. We'll have a civilized Sunday brunch, discuss our future and then have sex. "Listen, we'll talk later," I tell Lydia as I attempt to edge past her. "Dying to hear all the details about you and Rhys," I add as I frantically look for an escape route.

But I'm trapped. Wedged in by a waiter on one side and an actress on the other. I turn to find Vince is feet away, and he's definitely pissed.

"Mrs Rossi," he says once he's come to a stop a few feet away as I look for another avenue of escape. "Stop. Right. There."

I glance at Lydia and shrug just as she shrieks, "You married him!"

"Freaking Las Vegas, am I right?" I shrug again as if to express that I have zero accountability in this surprise wedding.

"When?" Lydia demands. "When did this happen? How did this happen? You only met him two weeks ago! Payton! And you didn't even invite me?"

Shit. "I would have," I say slowly because I would have. I didn't mean to exclude her, but it's not like it was planned. "If I'd known it was happening. I absolutely would have invited you. You'd have made a much better maid of honor than Canon, that's for sure. My hair was a mess and he didn't even tell me. The wedding photos are horrible."

"There are photos?"

"Yeah. I think they came with the package. Did they come with the package, Vince?" When I look at him I realize something. He called me Mrs Rossi. He looks like he wants to murder me, but he called me Mrs Rossi. He's never called me that before.

"When did this happen?" Lydia asks.

"Um, sometime after the auction but before the next morning. Somewhere in there. Things got a little crazy. I don't want to beat a dead horse about you missing it, but that night was a real good time."

"So why are you avoiding Vince now?" she asks. "Vince, also known as your husband. Why are you avoiding him if you're married?"

"Calm down. Everyone knows what happens in Vegas isn't legally binding." Just as soon as the judge signs off on that annulment it won't be legally anything. It'll just be undone.

"That's not a thing that is true," Lydia replies while Vince exhales and closes the remaining distance between us, placing a hand on my back in a very obvious attempt to physically hold onto me so I don't take off again.

"Enough. We need to talk," Vince says, and he doesn't appear to be in the mood for me to reschedule our talk until tomorrow, so I guess we're doing this now.

"Ugh. Talking is the worst." I groan. Unless... unless he wants to call me Mrs Rossi again? I liked that, very much. But why did he call me Mrs Rossi if he's not interested in being married? Just to get my attention? To remind me I'm only a temporary Mrs Rossi? Or is there something more going on here?

THIRTY-ONE

VINCE TAKES MY hand, his grip firm as if he's leaving no chance that I'll snatch my hand away and disappear into the crowd. His tug is firm as well, as he moves through the crowd towards the hall pulling me along with him. I think we're leaving, but he stops when we hit the casino floor. It's less crowded here but just as noisy. The machines are blaring and people are mingling and talking.

So I'm caught off guard when Vince presses me against the side of a twenty-five-cent slot machine and kisses me. Really kisses me. Hands on the side of my face, tongue down my throat, knee between my thighs kind of kissing. He doesn't even seem to care that we're in public and missing an invisibility cloak.

When his lips break from mine he's breathing heavily, his eyes locked on mine.

"Tell me again how it's fine that you were served with annulment papers ending this."

I guess he's got a real fixation with the words 'it's fine.'

"Sure," I reply. "As soon as you tell me how it's fine that your ex-girlfriend filed the paperwork for you."

His eyes widen and I want to yell 'haha, take that,

fucker,' but I refrain.

"What do you know about Gwen?"

Exactly the response every woman wants to hear.

I tug myself out of his embrace and give him the dirtiest look I can muster for a woman who was just kissed in a way that she thought was leading to an orgasm, not a fight.

"I know she's your ex-girlfriend. I know she works for you. I know she prepared the annulment paperwork."

"Okay." His brows rise in surprise, then he blows out a breath and pinches the bridge of his nose. "I can see how this looks to you."

"Yup." I pop the 'p' and cross my arms, glaring. Wait. "How does this look to me?" I ask just to make sure we're on the same page.

"Yes, Gwen and I used to date. Years ago, Payton. It's been over for years and it was barely anything to begin with. And yes, she works at my firm. And yes, I asked her to prepare the annulment paperwork for me because that's her speciality and I was drowning on prep for the case this week. But I can see how utterly stupid that was. Thoughtless. Inconsiderate."

"You can?" God, he's hard to argue with.

"I can. I'm sorry, Payton. I thought that was what you wanted when you ran out on me on Sunday. But by Tuesday it wasn't what I wanted, so I sent an email asking her not to file it while I figured it out. While I figured you out."

"You did?" Oh, God. He wants to figure me out. He does love me and this feels like hope blossoming in my chest.

"I did."

"So what happened? Does Gwen secretly still harbor feelings for you and she filed that paperwork anyway in a desperate attempt to break us up?" My eyes are wide as I visualize the scene.

"No, she went into labor." Vince is frowning at me like I'm nuts.

"Labor?"

"Not mine," he quickly interjects. "Before your overactive imagination flies off into Neverland. Not my kid. She married a tax attorney two years ago. I hadn't realized she was that close to maternity leave or I'd not have asked her to to deal with it in the first place. I honestly..." He pauses as if this is going to sound so bad he needs to mull the words over before he says them out loud. "I don't really pay that much attention to her. My firm is fairly large, I've got a lot of employees, between there and the club."

"You have a very nice website," I offer.

"You were stalking me on my website?" He smiles.

"Maybe. And I apologize for running out on you last Sunday. I really did have a meeting though."

"Yeah, with your essential oils life coach." Vince smirks as he runs his hand down my arm and pulls me close again.

"Canon told you that?" My cheeks flame in mortification. "Is nothing sacred with that guy?"

"Not much, no."

He kisses me again, one hand on my hip, holding me to him, the other cupping my jaw so he can angle my lips exactly how he wants them.

"You're impulsive," he says when he breaks off the kiss. "Hasty. You make rash decisions based on whatever amuses you at the moment."

"Those are all terrible, terrible traits," I agree. Because he's not wrong and I'm very self-aware. "But I'm also very self-aware. And I'm adaptable to change. I'm spontaneous and outgoing."

"How am I supposed to know if I can keep your attention? If this is real for you or a passing fad? If you'll change your mind in a month or a year?"

"I won't." I shake my head. "Not about you. I may be impulsive and a bit crazy and have questionable decision-making skills, but not about the really important things."

"You offered to share me, Payton. Remember? You offered to be some kind of alternate girlfriend number three," he reminds me.

"I changed my mind about that!"

He raises his brows as if this proves his point about my indecisiveness.

"I didn't know then that I was going to fall in love with you. Like crazy in love with you. The kind of love that terrifies me because everything I've ever been taught about love is that it's semi-permanent and in a constant state of flux. But I did and I do and I don't regret it. I'm willing to risk my heart on loving you."

"Good." He smiles a slow, easy smile that makes his eyes light up.

"What does that mean?"

"It means that I love you too. And I'll spend the rest of my life chasing you, if that's what I have to do. I'll do whatever it takes to keep your interest because I'm not living without you if you decide that fate or kismet or a Magic 8-Ball has determined that you should be with someone else."

"That's not how fate works, Vince. Kismet is a swan not a porcupine. I wasn't sure for a couple of days there, I worried that kismet might actually be a cunt, but it's not."

"I don't have any idea what you just said."

"Swans mate for life and porcupines just run around banging whoever they want to. But it's not important."

"Okay then," Vince replies as he envelops my hand in his and heads in the direction of the valet.

"Are we done talking? Because I still have more questions."

"We'll talk in the car."

THIRTY-TWO

"WHERE ARE WE going?"

It's not that I don't want to be with Vince, because I do. But we're currently driving out of town and it's feeling very murder-y because the only thing out of town in Las Vegas is the desert. Deserts, coyotes and wolves. Actually, I've got no idea what lives in the deserts outside of Las Vegas.

"It's a surprise."

"Exactly what a murderer would say," I mumble.

"God, Payton, your imagination." Vince just smiles and shakes his head.

We seem to be headed towards Red Rock, a national park on the outskirts of the city. I haven't been there yet because I'm not much of an outdoors girl. Especially outdoor areas with bears and stuff.

"Are there any bears in the desert? No, never mind. That doesn't sound right."

"No bears. Deer and bighorn sheep, mostly. Coyotes, of course."

Great.

We're quiet for a bit until I ask him what I really want to know.

"Tell me why you didn't tell me about all the charity stuff. Tell me why you'd let me think that strippers were your hobby."

247

"Maybe they are my hobby?"

"Vince." I sigh.

"My mother was a stripper, Payton. She worked her ass off removing her clothing so that I could have everything I needed. Little League and swimming lessons and tutors. Her life revolved around making sure I had everything I needed to succeeded, and I had no idea how difficult her life was."

"Of course you didn't, Vince, you were a kid."

"She died in a car accident while I was in my senior year of college. Fell asleep at the wheel and drove off the road. And you know why? Do you know why she died? Because she was exhausted from working three jobs. She was working three jobs because she'd gotten too old to dance for money and there was no exit plan for her, Payton. She was a forty-something woman without a job skill that would pay her a living wage. And I was a college kid who still didn't have a fucking clue what it takes to make it in the world when no one is helping you."

"So you made an exit plan," I say softly, suddenly very touched at what drives him. At this tribute to his mother. "You bought a club and made an exit plan because it's too late to help your mom, but you can help these women. The scholarships and childcare reimbursement and the good insurance plans."

"Fuck, Canon is a wordy bitch, isn't he?"

"Yup."

"So." He blows out a breath and changes lanes, speeding past a slow-moving sedan. "Now you know. I don't do all that stuff because I'm a good person. I do it because I'm fucked up."

"You're the least-fucked up strip club owner I've ever known."

"You only think that because you love me." He reaches over to squeeze my leg and I think it's all going to be okay. I think whatever happens, we're going to be okay.

We're still headed towards Red Rock and I'm sure that's where we're going until Vince turns, the car slowing to a stop in front of a large iron gate. Vince hits a button on his visor and a moment later it swings open and we proceed through into what appears to be a remote gated home community. Acreage lots and an excess of trees. It's very lush, so a lot of care to plant things that will thrive in this climate was taken. Manicured lawns surrounded by desert-friendly gravel and rock to break up the landscape. It takes another two minutes of winding through this development before Vince pulls off the road onto a gravel drive leading to... nowhere. There's nothing here, just a huge vacant lot. Several acres appear to separate the closest neighbors, but I can see the dull glow of lights on either side. Straight ahead is nothing but a direct view of Red Rock and... a tent?

Vince turns off the engine and circles the hood of the car to open my door. It's almost chilly, for Nevada, the weather having dipped down to the fifties with the setting of the sun. Vince puts his arm around me and walks me in the direction of the tent, making sure I don't trip in my heels.

It's way more than a tent though. It's a full-fledged glamping setup. The tent flap is zipped back to reveal a freaking full-sized bed inside and I'm guessing that's a real mattress, not a blow-up. A chandelier is hanging from the branch of a tree covered in fairy lights. A fire pit has been created out of the perfect selection of rocks with a fire already crackling inside. Before the fire pit are two chairs, with something resembling a small tree stump set between, but it's too perfect to be real so I'm sure it came from a home design store. On top of the stump are all of the necessary bits to make s'mores. A stack of graham crackers, chocolate bars and marshmallows rest inside of a glass-domed cake stand, with two perfect sticks for roasting marshmallows resting beside the cake stand.

I walk closer and that's when I notice one end of one of the sticks has been painted in pink sparkly nail polish.

Just like the one I had as a kid but never got to use. He's recreated the camp trip I missed. Well, a way better recreation. Better because he's here and better because this is more glamping than camping, which is perfect because it was really only the s'mores and the badge I was interested in. I'm going to have to ask him who he hired to pull this off because I'm impressed. This wasn't something he did himself, this required a team of people and a forklift of some kind to hang all those lights. And a generator, Jesus.

"You remembered," I say, picking up the stick and running it between my fingers.

"I remember everything you tell me," he responds. His hands are in his pockets and he's watching me very carefully as I turn the stick over in my hands.

"Where are we? What is this place?"

"I own this lot," he says. "I've owned it for damn close to a decade."

"But it's empty." I shift my eyes around even though I know a home isn't about to suddenly appear before me. And this is residential. It's not like he's been keeping this lot for dirt biking or whatever people would keep land for.

"I was going to build on it. Real estate is a great investment, so I thought I'd build a home."

"Why didn't you? Ten years is a long time to wait for permits."

He smiles at my joke, a small tug of his lips that makes me smile in return. Then his expression turns serious. "Because I was waiting for you."

Oh, God. Oh, God! The way he looks at me when he says that, holy hell. The swans in my stomach just threw up because I think my husband might be about to propose to me.

"I hired an architect. Had plans drawn up, the whole bit. I drove out here one day after they'd staked off an outline of the house, to make sure the windows were going to line up with the view in the way I wanted. That the kitchen would open up in the exact right spot to the backyard. That kind of shit."

"So what happened?"

"This little girl came over." He laughs when he says it, glancing around at the empty lot. "A Girl Trooper, with a wagon full of cookies. She left the wagon in the street with her mom as she ran up that shitty gravel drive to my nonexistent house asking if I wanted to buy cookies." He smiles again, shaking his head at the memory. "And I thought to myself, 'Vince, what in the hell are you doing? You're building a family house without a family. You're building a house your future wife might not like. She should be a part of designing the house, building it.' So I scrapped the project, but I kept the lot."

"After you bought every box of cookies that kid had."

"God, the entire fucking wagon full." He smiles,

remembering. "I want you to be the wife I build a house with. Right here, if you don't hate this property."

"I don't hate it," I whisper, shaking my head back and forth to reiterate my thoughts on this location.

"I don't want to fast-pass with you, Payton. I don't want to skip anything, I want to experience every moment."

"You do?"

"I do. You and your vivid imagination have gotten me thinking."

"I have?"

"You have. And I want it all. I want to stand in line with you. I want to experience life with you, Payton, all of it. Every single thing. Even when the dog throws up at three AM and one of us has to get out of bed to deal with it."

"We have a dog?" I ask.

"We do." He nods. "And kids. The dog destroys one of their science projects the night before it's due, but it's fine because after a lot of tears we stay up all night fixing it. We drink a bottle of wine and laugh about what an asshole our dog is."

"We have kids?"

"A bunch of kids." Vince smiles and I think he must be right. I'll be knocked up around the clock as long as he looks at me like that. Then he pauses. "At least I think we do. Do we?"

"We definitely do. We would make really beautiful babies, it was the first thing I noticed about you."

"Was it?" His lips twitch in amusement.

"Mmm-hmm," I murmur, biting my lip to hold back a ridiculously sized smile. I like this, all of it. It's nice to have someone else do the imagining for once. Really nice.

"We have a date night, every Tuesday," he continues. "We can't do the weekends because of all the soccer and ballet and that one kid who insists on taking a sixteen-week course in ceramics, which is only available clear across town, at eight AM on Saturdays."

I nod, because that's exactly how I'd imagine it too.

"Our babysitter cancels on our anniversary"—he shrugs—"but it's fine because we've got all those kids and we're tired. So we stay home and order pizza and watch something on Netflix."

"No." I shake my head, fighting back a smile. "We never miss an anniversary because Canon is our backup sitter. We leave him with our gaggle of children while we go to dinner because we like to live on the edge like that."

"Agreed." Vince nods. "Lydia would be too logical a choice to fill in. We like the messy choice."

"We love the messy choice. We'd come home to at least one kid with gum in their hair and a kitten we didn't own when we left."

Vince smiles and nods. "At least one kitten. Maybe three. They'd be matching kittens and it'd take us a week to figure out there were three of them."

"Or something worse, like a drum set for toddlers."

"Fucking Canon." Vince shakes his head.

"So how do we get all that?" I ask, because imagining is fun, but reality is a lot tougher. Is he really committed to forever?

"It won't be the easiest thing we've ever done," Vince answers. "We'll have to put the work in. Every day."

"I like the sound of us."

"It'll be easier for me, obviously."

"Why is that? Because you're less crazy than me?" I suck my bottom lip into my mouth, worried he still thinks I'm nuts.

"No. It'll be easier for me because I get the better end of the deal; I get you. Every day I get to spend with you is a win for me."

"Oh." He's doing that thing where he looks at me, in that way like I fascinate him. In that way like he loves me. Every crazy bit of me. "So you want to stay married to me? A random girl who maybe sorta tricked you into marrying her while you were drunk?"

"I'll tell you a secret, Payton."

"What's that?"

"I wasn't that drunk."

"You weren't?"

"I was sober enough to know better, and just drunk enough not to care. I was captivated with you, and yes, it was the most irresponsible and out-of-character thing I've ever done in my life, but fuck it, I wanted to see where it was going to lead."

"You could have just let me get the tattoo and asked me out like a normal person."

"What kind of story is that for our grandchildren?"

I nod, because that's a very valid point.

"So, Mrs Rossi, do you agree to stay married to me? Through the good times and the bad. Through the dogs who will vomit, and the kids who will fight and the babysitters who will cancel. Through all the things that haven't happened yet and that we'll never see coming. What do you say? Do you vow to stick it out with me and stay married till death do us part?"

"Because you're in love with me?"

"I'm so in love with you," he responds as he pulls something out of his pocket and drops to one knee. It's a ring, and it's beautiful. A large round center diamond surrounded by a halo of tiny diamonds. It sparkles in the light of the fire and I love it, but I love that he picked it out and made the gesture even more. "Love is a word that means infatuation and lust and respect and devotion," he says as he slips the ring onto my finger. "Tenderness and affection and friendship and passion. I feel all of those things for you, Payton, and I'll spend the rest of my life showing you just how much if you'll agree to stay and be mine."

"I'd legiterally like nothing more."

EPILOGUE

VINCE

HAPPY WIFE, HAPPY life.

I'm an intelligent man so I live my life by this philosophy. Luckily for me, it's not hard because if the name Payton had a definition it would be 'happy.' Characterized by joy and delight.

I'm not sure what I've done to deserve her, but I'll spend forever keeping her. I worried in the beginning that she'd grow bored. That she was too young. That she couldn't possibly be as serious about me as I was about her.

Ridiculous as it was to feel serious about someone you'd known two weeks.

I met her at noon on a Saturday.

Within twenty-four hours we were married, and she'd left me in the honeymoon suite we'd only partially christened. Without a word or a phone number or a note on the nightstand.

I wasn't in love with her that morning.

I went to her apartment anyway, just to talk. To make sure she was okay. To make sure she ate. I slept with her because she was sober and because she asked. The bossy way she told me exactly how she wanted me to fuck her, but then stripped out of her clothing with no finesse at all was so beguiling to me.

The Tennessee driver's license in her handbag was the first inkling I had that something was happening between us, for me at least. *Don't go,* I thought. *Jesus Christ, whatever you do, do not leave the state.* Not because it would make the annulment difficult, but because I hated the idea of her being so far away. Yet less than an hour later she was bolting again, running out the door of her own apartment with her bra in her hand and some ridiculous talk of having to be somewhere other than postcoital with me.

I wasn't in love with her by Sunday afternoon. Or hell, maybe I was. I was still grappling with what had possessed me to marry her in the first place. I was casual drunk, not stupid drunk. Yet when her eyes lit up with the idea of getting a tiger tattooed onto her ass there was no way I was allowing that. "What's the B?" I asked. We'd spent the entire evening making choices based on A or B options, surely there was a B to getting a tattoo. When she quipped, "Getting married," somewhere in my normally practical and orderly mind a voice whispered, *Yeah, do that.*

I love a good deed. What better deed could there be than rescuing her ass from a tiger tat?

Weak. It's a weak excuse. It was always a weak excuse. Temporary insanity is the only thing that justifies marrying her that night. Temporary insanity, or fate.

I was leaning towards temporary insanity on Monday morning when I started the annulment paperwork. Paperwork so irrelevant I passed it off to Gwen to handle. Gwen, ex-girlfriend so irrelevant it hadn't occurred to me that it might be improper or offensive to have her handle it. She was always more of a friend than anything else. She completed it without judgement, bringing it discreetly to my office and placing it on my desk while rubbing her pregnant stomach with her free hand. Gwen was a nice girl but I was never in love with her. We had some charitable work in common, law and not much else. Our relationship hadn't been much more than co-workers with benefits, which wasn't enough for her, so she'd dumped me and found the tax attorney she'd married. Nice guy. I'd felt nothing but happy for her, the way you'd be happy for anyone.

On Monday night I left work with the annulment papers, intent on stopping at Payton's to discuss them with her. I could've let her figure it out when she got served, but I'm not an asshole. I could spare an hour to explain the process to her so she wasn't blindsided. That's all it was. The weekend of revelry and foolish choices was over.

So why did I stop for groceries so I could make her dinner while we talked? I've got no idea.

Fate or insanity?

When she swung the door open with a huge grin and a joke about how I'd been avoiding her, something shifted in me. She'd already changed into pajamas—the least sexy or seductive set of pajamas possible. She wasn't expecting me, or if she was she wasn't planning a seduction. Or possibly this was just Payton. Possibly this was how she always was.

In that moment it'd been easy to imagine a lifetime of her—just like this. Welcoming me home without makeup, her hair gathered messily on her head, wearing pajamas and teasing me.

I didn't hate the idea of it.

She questioned why I was bringing her dinner and

I nearly answered, "Because I liked talking to you," but the thought surprised me so I made a deflective comment about multitasking instead.

I'm not sure I can pinpoint the exact moment in the evening that I stopped wanting to talk to her about those papers and started wanting to know more about her instead.

She was such a mystery to me at that point. Was she just looking to have a good time? Or was she looking for something more? She'd propositioned me for sex, married me and then run out on me. Twice. But that night, sitting at her kitchen table in a pair of cotton pajamas, she bit her lip and offered me health insurance—as an incentive to stay with her. Offered me some kind of marriage of convenience, as if she wanted this to last in whatever form she could get it. She was such a contradiction. Confident with a hint of insecurity. Aggressive with a dash of adorable. Crazy with a silver lining that was all heart.

So I stayed. Talked to her. Slept with her again. Every night.

I couldn't stop myself. I lived within walking distance of my office—it was the only reason I picked my apartment—yet every evening I'd find myself in my car driving to Payton's apartment.

She liked me, I knew that much. She liked me even when she thought I was a strip club owner who might be in need of healthcare or tax relief. She liked the idea of being married, but was terrified of it at the same time. So she was trying me on, like a sample. And I was falling in love with her.

She said she was falling in love with me, but could I trust that? A week into our relationship? Into our marriage? Payton was a spontaneous wildfire with an overactive imagination.

And I loved her.

Then she got served with the annulment paperwork and she shut down before she'd even talked to me about it. Paperwork that was never meant to be sent, but instead of trusting her instincts about us, about me, clammed up. She told me later that her plan was to woo me once the annulment was processed. She thought we'd date and she'd woo me into loving her back.

But there wasn't a chance that was happening because I already loved her and I wasn't letting her go.

I asked her if she wanted a re-do. A real wedding, as it were. A dress and flowers and a fancy dinner with all her friends and family present. She looked at me with an expression akin to horror and said, "God, no. Please don't make me do that."

When I finished laughing she kissed me and said the wedding we'd already had was the only one she wanted, and all she'd ever need.

"You might regret it later," I warned. She promised if she ever felt the desire for a wedding re-do she'd let me know.

She did request a honeymoon re-do and I happily obliged.

I took her to the Maldives, to one of those resorts with private thatch-roofed overwater bungalows. Ten days of relaxation, sex and not a single tan line on Payton.

It was heaven, but every day since has been just as great. Two years of viewing the world though a Payton lens and I'm not sure how I ever coped without her.

She moved into my cold and lifeless condo at first

because it made the most sense for both of us. Not surprisingly, it didn't feel cold and lifeless with her in it. Still, I don't miss it. Last month we moved into our new home, the one we constructed on the lot where I'd asked her to stay, where I'd laid out a fantasy vision of our future, telling her I was all in.

The reality is better.

The garage door slides up as I pull into the driveway. Some fancy contraption linking my car to the automatic door. I park and I've got to admit, it's satisfying as fuck to have a home. I've never owned a home before. I've never lived in a home before. Growing up it was apartments. Once I had money it was nicer apartments and then the condo. I wish my mom could be here to see it, but I know she'd be proud of me and that gives me peace.

My lovely wife is in the kitchen when I enter the house through the garage. She's standing at the island countertop, making a list of something on a notepad. She still works in event planning at the Windsor, but she's got quite a side business planning events on her own. She looks up at my arrival and grins, giving me an enthusiastic kiss and a hello. I make it ten feet past the kitchen before I stop.

It's an open-concept home so I can see Payton from where I'm standing. I can also see a baby. I walk closer, just to be sure my eyes aren't deceiving me or she hasn't purchased one of those very expensive dolls they use for high-school classes to terrify teenagers out of procreating.

It's a real baby. Asleep, but very real. It's sitting in some kind of bouncy seat contraption in the middle of our family room.

We don't have a baby.

We don't have any friends who have a baby.

I glance back to Payton, but she's ignoring me as she jots away at her list.

"Payton, where did this baby come from?"

"Oh!" Payton looks up, an expression of excitement on her face. She claps her hands together, as if she cannot contain her enthusiasm, as she abandons her list to join me. "She's ours now. Do you like her?"

Fuck.

"Payton Elizabeth, where did you get this baby?"

"I'm just messing with you." She rolls her eyes and shakes her head as if I'm so gullible. "She belongs to the next-door neighbor and I'm not sampling her without permission, so you can wipe that look off your face right now."

"Why is she here?" I think it's a she. She's wearing a baby headband with a giant pink bow.

"Well, I was helping plan Lucy's birthday party," Payton begins.

"Who is Lucy?"

"The baby. I wouldn't have chosen it myself, but it's a lovely name. I was thinking option A, Annabel, or option B, Joseph. What do you think?"

Good Lord, where to start. I look at her carefully, assessing.

"Are you pregnant, Payton?"

"Not yet, but I was thinking maybe I should be? That maybe it's time to try?"

"You were thinking this based on a couple of hours of baby-sampling?"

"Oh, don't be ridiculous. Lucy's been here for five minutes. Her mother just ran out to meet the school bus."

"Okay, so how did you come to the conclusion

that we're ready to be parents?" I think we're ready, but I'd like to hear her thoughts. I always like hearing her thoughts.

"I was thinking it might be time to try because you're very elderly."

I side-eye her.

"So we should probably start having kids."

"That's up to you, Payton. Whenever you're ready." I'm ready, elderliness aside.

"We'll want them all out of college by the time you retire," Payton continues. "And you know at least one of them will be that kid who's on the six-year plan. And another will want to go to graduate school or become a lawyer. That'll probably be Annabel, she'll be a lawyer just like her daddy."

"How considerate of you to think all this through." I pull her close to me and she yelps, not expecting it. Then I kiss her. I'd fuck her over the back of our new sofa, but there's a baby here. The restraint's good practice, I tell myself, because I don't think we're going to have long in this house, just the two of us.

It's fine. I had the builder soundproof the master bedroom. It's not that we're especially kinky but a family home means a couple of decades of living with people who never want to hear us have sex.

Which reminds me.

"How does the A or B game work when one's a girl name and one's a boy name? You get your pick either way."

"Uh, I don't see how that's true."

I can't wait for her to explain this to me. I fight a smile and bury my face in her neck, breathing her in before I ask, "How's that?"

"You get to decide which sperm you impregnate

me with, so it's really your choice."

"Well played, Mrs Rossi." I laugh now because I love bantering with her. "We'll start practicing as soon as the sample goes home."

"Good idea," my wife agrees with an eager nod and a sneaky grab at my ass.

"Option A, you tied to our new headboard with the convenient iron rails? Or option B, you on top riding cowgirl?"

"C, both," she answers and this time she smacks my ass before she walks over to pick up the baby.

I'm not sure how I got so lucky. If it was fate or synchronicity or kismet or coincidence, but I'm thankful all the same. Because every day with Payton is the best day of my life.

ACKNOWLEDGMENTS

Readers, THANK YOU! I am forever grateful each & every time you choose to read my words. It humbles me to my very soul. Thank you, thank you, thank you.

RJ Locksley, thank you for putting up with my crazy turnaround times on these edits!!!

Thank you to Letitia Hasser for another delicious cover & to Kari March for my gorgeous teasers. Erik Gevers for the paperback formatting!

Getting ARC's out the door & promotions lined up is no small task. Many thanks to Candi Kane & Sarah Piechuta for their help in managing the chaos.

Jean Siska, Melissa Panio-Peterson, Marie Jocke, Lydia Rella, thank you for everything you do!

Staci Hart, Liv Morris, Kayti McGee, Amy Daws, Raine Miller, BJ Harvey, Sierra Simone, Laurelin Paige, Jade West, it's a joy to be on this author journey with each of you.

ABOUT THE AUTHOR

Jana Aston likes cats, big coffee cups and books about billionaires who deflower virgins. She wrote her debut novel while fielding customer service calls about electrical bills, and she's ever grateful for the fictional gynecologist in Wrong that readers embraced so much she was able to make working in her pajamas a reality.

Jana's novels have appeared on the NYT, USA Today and Wall Street Journal bestsellers list, some multiple times. She likes multiples.

SOCIAL MEDIA

I have a reader group on Facebook & I'd love to see you there! If you're into that sort of thing, please join us in the Grind Me Café:
bit.ly/GrindMeCafe

Facebook page Jana Aston
bit.ly/FBJanaAston

Twitter @janaaston
bit.ly/TwitterJanaAston

Instagram JanaAston
bit.ly/IGJanaAston

Website
www.janaaston.com

Signed Paperbacks
bit.ly/SignedJana

If you prefer to avoid social media & have my release news sent straight to your mailbox, sign up for my newsletter here:
bit.ly/NewsletterJana

ALSO BY JANA ASTON